Before the Leaves Fall

CLARE O'DEA

Fairlight Books

First published by Fairlight Books 2025

Fairlight Books
Summertown Pavilion, 18–24 Middle Way, Oxford,
OX2 7LG

A CIP catalogue record for this book is available from the British
Library.

1 2 3 4 5 6 7 8 9 10

ISBN 978-1-914148-82-8

www.fairlightbooks.com

Printed and bound in Great Britain

Cover Design © Rebecca Fish

MIX
Paper | Supporting
responsible forestry
FSC
www.fsc.org   FSC® C018072

For my daughters

What do we live for, if it is not to make
life less difficult to each other?
—*Middlemarch*, George Eliot

I

Ruedi

He wasn't doing it for the money, that much was clear. So why? Maria would have had an opinion on that. 'Well, Maria?'

His wife looked on from her position on the wall as Ruedi tore open the single-portion packet of rösti and squeezed the slimy contents into the pan.

Ruedi liked to slip his daughter Alessandra a few francs when he saw her. So it would be good to do that without the mental arithmetic. In that way, the extra money would be welcome. 'You know what I mean, Maria.' Retiring early to look after her had taken a serious bite out of his pension. 'No reproaches, my love.'

Her warm smile held strong. One of the best photos he had of her from that last year, taken on a day trip they made to Brienz. It was a day of the most extraordinary warm wind. They'd got a table on a restaurant terrasse right on the lake, and the waiters rushed around taking down the yellow parasols before they were blown away. Maria and he held on to their glasses as the tablecloths fluttered dangerously. She had that girlish gleam in her eye; she was enjoying the drama. Afterwards he pushed her along the lakeshore path and they took photos of the view and each other. All was well.

Ruedi broke up the potato mix with a wooden spoon and turned up the heat. There were other reasons people did things. For love, for glory, for posterity. To be useful. The health insurance magazine that kept arriving unbidden had surprisingly good articles. There were six pillars of brain health, he had read this morning. Or was it seven? One boiled down to being useful.

You had to make life interesting for yourself, wasn't that it? Nobody was going to put together a programme for you. Last winter, he realised his life was no longer interesting. The dog was gone; no question of replacing him at this stage. Ruedi couldn't give his heart away again. Alessandra only wanted to see him when she needed something. Without Maria to care for, the routine was quiet, so quiet. The ad in the Depart newsletter had jumped out at him. And here he was, six months later, fully trained and ready to take on his first client solo. He placed his hand on his stomach to quell the swirling feeling.

Sitting down to his rösti, fried egg and sliced tomato, he reached for the Maggi bottle and scattered a few drops over his meal. You could do worse for lunch under five francs, he thought. Being thrifty came naturally to Ruedi – he had learned from the best. He was proud not to be taking any medication either, which made him almost a freak among his age group. Maria had had rows of pills to take. Muscle relaxants, anti-spasm tablets, painkillers, blood pressure tablets, anti-depressants, food supplements, even medical cannabis for a time.

Careful not to get any stains on the plastic folder, he opened the file and read the information again. There wasn't much to go on. Born in 1936, so that would make her eighty-six. Margrit Brändli had been a member of Depart since 2000. He wondered what had given her the nudge back then. Often it's someone else's situation that prompts people to sign up for membership. A situation that provokes sympathy or dread. For others, it's a routine task on the post-retirement to-do list.

He read Mrs Brändli's list of co-morbidities. A heavy load to carry by any measure, and at eighty-six, poor thing. Her care home was called Sonnmatt. Well, every village has a sunny meadow – it might not be false advertising. Would she see that he was out of his depth? Was he out of his depth? According to Carmen he was ready, as she had reminded him again this morning by text. Shadowing Carmen had been a most fascinating experience. She had a gift.

The food had fixed the swirling in his stomach, and now he felt a tightness in his throat. He held out his hands. Steady as a surgeon's. The children from the upper floors clattered down the stairs past his door. They all left together without fail at one fifteen. Ruedi loved the sound of their voices, but he was shy with them and their parents and never seemed to get past smiles and hellos. He went to the window and watched until they had safely crossed the road. His favourite kids were the Portuguese brother and sister. The boy was about ten and his little sister five. He waited patiently with her whenever she stopped to look at insects or pick up leaves. He must have been under strict instructions to stay close to her all the way to and from school. Ruedi found his loyalty delightful.

Ruedi fetched a little square of paper from the wooden holder made by Florian in school. It sat on what used to be the telephone table in the hall until Alessandra had convinced him that he could live without a landline.

While his coffee brewed, he looked up the route on the SBB app again and wrote down all the connections. Alessandra had trained him. Every time she came to see him, she had a new skill to teach. It was kind of her, but a little wearing.

He was lucky to have the bus stop almost outside his door. After a thirteen-minute journey, he would arrive at Bern main station and, according to the little walking symbol, it would take six minutes to get to platform one. Seven stops on the regional line and he would arrive at the village, with a four-minute wait for a bus to whisk him two stops to the care home. The coffee sputtered on the hob. In a little over an hour, he would be there, fifteen minutes early for the appointment.

Standing at the hob, Ruedi fetched a cup, sugar and coffee cream, all within arm's reach. Maria had complained about their old-style cafetière. Could they not get a modern machine like everyone else? She always praised the coffee in other people's homes, looking pointedly at Ruedi. Finally, he had bought a nice little machine for Christmas, but she was too ill for coffee by the evening of the twenty-fourth, too ill for anything, and he returned it to the shop, unopened, in January. A small regret, but it niggled.

He went back to the window and took his coffee standing up. Too much looking in: that's what happens when you spend so much time alone. Look out, he urged himself, look out.

The hydrangea between the apartment blocks was in bloom, and its blowsy blue flowers curtsied in the breeze. Behind the buildings, he could see a tractor raking the freshly cut hay into rows. The forecast was good for the next few days. He felt the urge to hold a rake in his hands, to be out there all afternoon with his hands occupied and his mind free. Maybe it was time for a visit to the village. But not today: today was for Mrs Brändli, her cares and her reasons. The next bus was his.

2

Margrit

The pig was coming to visit today. No doubt Nadja thought this was her trump card, but Margrit was the last person to be charmed by a pig, unlike the others whose chatter over breakfast reminded her of children on the morning of a school trip. Margrit had an ongoing battle with the social activities woman, who seemed to take it personally that Margrit was the only resident who boycotted everything she organised. What Nadja didn't understand was that Margrit was not meant to be here. This was not her kind of place, and what Nadja with her big teeth considered exciting was not Margrit's kind of fun.

She'd had her fun. Margrit's kind of fun was dancing, preferably to big band music in a big hall late at night when everyone was past caring, throwing their young limbs around wildly and twisting their hips for joy. And the parties they threw before the kids came along, plenty of drinking and laughing, ham pastries in the oven, and Frederic on the piano. What she wouldn't give to watch him play one more time.

The cleaner came out of Margrit's room and nodded at her, still sitting there in the alcove in the corridor.

'All finished,' she said. '*Picobello.*'

Margrit respected the woman for her lack of cheerfulness. It was a welcome relief in this place.

'So, you're not meeting the pig?' the cleaner asked.

'No, not meeting the pig. I have a human visiting this afternoon.' Margrit was rewarded with a rare smile.

'A human.' The cleaner chuckled as she wheeled her cart away.

The phone bleated unanswered at reception, the door buzzed and clicked on the dementia wing around the corner, and from the dining room came the sound of plates and cutlery being roughly stacked into plastic trays. Someone was calling plaintively, and another voice was crying. A carer walked by briskly, too taken with her phone for a greeting. When Margrit was sure the corridor was empty, she gripped the walker hard and hauled herself upright. She waited a few breaths to steady herself before she released the brake.

Margrit's legs were lost, encased in these thick alien legs stretched taut with fluid, the papery skin full of ugly blotches. With baby steps, she made her way diagonally across to her door. The cleaner (what was her name again, Christine, Christina, Corinne?) had left it wedged open. It took Margrit some careful manoeuvring with her walker to force the wedge out from under the door and to close it behind her. Safely inside, she kept moving and managed to close the window before circling back and landing on her chair with a heavy bump. Her son Peter had paid for this wonderful chair and she was glad to have it. With a few touches on the control panel, she had herself nicely set up with her legs raised and back reclined. She pulled the shawl from her bed and draped it over her bulky form. A little rest was in order before the Depart man arrived at three.

Sleep didn't come, but Margrit entered a state of wandering in her memories that allowed her body to relax completely. Better this than the nonsense Nadja was peddling, yoga and meditation. Margrit had been caught in a talk about mindfulness the other day because her legs were acting up, and she hadn't been able to leave the day room quickly enough. You had to be vigilant in this place. Nadja even had the fit residents doing tai chi, or some version of the movements, in the garden once a week. A silly-looking spectacle.

The pull of the past was strong. Margrit had eight decades and more to choose from, but she returned most often to her youth, and the years when the children were small. Today she remembered the day her brother Marcel brought home his Indian girlfriend who spoke not a word of German, let alone Swiss German. Margrit's father had driven into the village to collect them from the bus stop, and her mother, Vreni, was in a state of high anxiety. At the last minute, she discovered an old mustard stain on the white tablecloth and rushed to clear and reset the table with the stain repositioned up at her end. She wouldn't let Margrit help because Margrit mentioned she'd been having false contractions.

After hearing the doctor's explanation, Margrit wasn't worried; she was more fascinated than anything whenever the muscles around her belly clenched tight. It was a reminder that something momentous was going to happen and that she really would have her own baby soon, in six weeks if all went according to plan. Sitting in the good room watching her mother flit about, she remembered being suffused with a deep sense of well-being and an awareness of her maternal power.

'Everything is ready now. Come, sit with me for a minute before they arrive.' She patted the sofa beside her.

Vreni stopped and looked tenderly at her daughter. She'd got her hair set the day before in the new hairdressers in the village, and Margrit thought she looked quite well, considering.

'Do you need anything, love?' Vreni asked.

'No, I'm fine – I have my glass of syrup here. I just want you to relax. Sit down. And tell me more about this girl, Usha.'

Vreni clasped her hands together and surveyed the table one more time.

'It's a nice name, I suppose. Educated in London, the job in Geneva. I don't know, I get the impression she's a high society kind of girl. What will she make of us?' Vreni gestured around the room as if it were lacking something important. The bright new lino made everything else look a bit darker and shabbier.

'She's not some kind of inspector though, Mami. Just a girl alone in a foreign country. Marcel wouldn't fall for someone high and mighty, don't worry.'

Vreni sat on the settee beside Margrit. 'Do you know what I like about you?'

Margrit held on to her smile, eager to hear the compliment.

'A lot of things, really. But what I see today is how composed you are. Nothing knocks you off balance. It's lovely to see.'

'If I'm strong, I got it from you.'

'I don't think that's how it works. People come into the world with their own powers – just you wait and see.' She placed her warm hand gently on Margrit's bump.

They sat in silence until the others came, enjoying a moment of perfect peace and mutual appreciation. Margrit would forever be glad that she had reached this level of harmony with her mother before she lost her.

At the gathering afterwards, Marcel kept the conversation going, switching in and out of English like a professional. But that's what he was now, a man of the world, a more open and excited version of himself, with stories of Geneva this and Geneva that. There was even talk of a position in New York. Margrit was happy for him. There was some confusion about Usha being a vegetarian which Vreni thought could be overcome by persuasion. Everyone loved her boiled ham with potato salad. How could you skip the best part of the meal? In all the years Usha was part of their family, the same debate took place at the table in Mendenswil. But Vreni pounced on anyone who made disparaging remarks about her daughter-in-law. She would not tolerate any barbed comments about foreigners or dark skin. Nobody was cleverer or more cultured than Usha, in her eyes.

Mami, Marcel, Usha – they had brought so much to Margrit's life. All long gone. It would be nice to think they could be together again sitting around a celestial table, but Margrit didn't believe any of that. She'd appreciated their times together in this world. That was what mattered.

Voices drifted in from the garden, actual laughter, and Margrit realised she was fully awake. The doctor the other day had asked her if she felt troubled, and he was so wide of the mark she wanted to shake him. She felt more tranquil than she had in years. She felt a heightened sense of clarity about everything. Not a million miles removed from Nadja's mindfulness talk, to be honest.

The consultation was for the doctor's report to send to Depart. She knew they would be trying to figure out if she was depressed and needed some other intervention. She could see that the doctor took her choice as a personal failure. *It's not about you, dear.* That's what she wanted to say to him, but it sounded patronising, so she had just smiled a benign old-lady smile.

3

Ruedi

Sitting on the regional train, Ruedi enjoyed the luxury of being a passenger, which still felt like a treat, even a decade after he'd worked his last shift for the SBB. As he watched the countryside roll by, it was the houses that interested him the most. Each house told a story, made a statement to the world about the lot of its inhabitants. Here lives a happy family, here lives a lonely old widower in need of help, here live hard workers with no time for frippery. Some houses were even graced with actual statements, quotes of thanks to God painted on the gables.

He felt his phone vibrate in his shoulder bag: a laptop bag minus a laptop, it performed the task of a handbag or briefcase without being feminine or old-fashioned. Alessandra's tip. Like a little attention-seeking animal that phone was. He fished his reading glasses out of his shirt pocket.

A message from Alessandra. He knew the system now. If he opened the message, she would know he'd seen and read it. From then on, the clock would be ticking as she waited for his response. Not the most patient person in his life. He really should be focusing on Mrs Brändli now. But he could just take a peek at the opening sentence to satisfy his curiosity. He unlocked the phone and opened the app.

Papi, something has come up and I need...

Need, an irresistible word to a parent. Reluctantly, Ruedi tapped on the message.

Papi, something has come up and I need your help. Crisis at work, long story. I have to attend a meeting in the school this eve. Can u come have dinner with Florian and wait for me? Don't want to leave him alone for too long.

Ruedi made a noise of irritation, like a short gasp, and the woman opposite froze as she noticed, realised he wasn't communicating with her, pretended she hadn't noticed in the first place, and switched back to pressing matters on her own phone.

Alessandra and Florian. They should be the two closest people in his life, but he didn't fully enjoy their company. Alessandra had a good heart. At least he hoped she did. But she was a person who thrived on drama and clashed with others frequently and, in his opinion, unnecessarily. She seemed to seek out conflict. The same prickly mentality had run through Maria's personality, like veins in marble. But it never dominated with his wife. In Alessandra's case, the prickliness had taken over. Meanwhile she lavished affection on her twelve-year-old son, to an unnatural degree. Almost a grown boy and she still cuddled him all the time. And as a result, he acted the baby. It set Ruedi's teeth on edge.

The first irritation out of the way, Ruedi knew he would naturally say yes. Alessandra wouldn't ask if she wasn't stuck. She didn't like people to judge her. He understood. And it would only be a small dose of them if he could leave again soon after her return.

OK, I can be there by 7pm. His responses were too blunt, she often complained. He added a sign-off. *All the best.* It looked ridiculous, but he knew the importance of compromise.

Really? Florian usually eats at 6.30. Can u not come earlier?

Ruedi composed himself by looking out of the window again. A field of deer appeared and was gone in a flash. Lovely creatures.

On way to an appointment now. Will do my best.

He didn't want her to know about Sonnmatt, about Mrs Brändli, his role in Depart, any of it. You never knew when Alessandra was going to have a personal or political objection to something. Even a casual remark could set her off. He turned off the data coverage on his phone, another one of Alessandra's useful tips. Next stop, Maggenried. Ruedi gathered his things into his laptop bag and left his fellow passenger in peace.

The home was indeed on the edge of a meadow. An angular 1980s building with metal trimmings in primary yellow, it was large considering the size of the village Ruedi had just driven through on the bus. Probably served a wider area. There was certainly no shortage of infirm elderly people in this part of the world. He lingered in the car park, checking his papers one more time so that he looked like he was on official business. Lavender and rose bushes filled the raised beds around the perimeter of the car park. An old stone water trough crammed tight with geraniums stood at the main entrance. Ruedi made his way towards the concentration of pink and red.

Inside, he was immediately aware of the uniquely stuffy air of a nursing home, different to a regular hospital or any other medical setting. Even the flowers on the front desk looked trapped and melancholy. An elderly man sat in a winged chair near the entrance. Ruedi greeted him and the man impatiently replied: 'Are you the fellow with the pig?'

Nonplussed, Ruedi hit the bell on the desk, feeling like a character from an old comedy sketch. Within ten seconds a woman wearing a pink medical jacket appeared. She spoke first to the old man.

'There's no point in waiting there. They're all in the back garden. Susanna announced that at breakfast, meet in the back garden. Maybe you didn't hear?'

'I can hear perfectly well, thank you.' The man got up, took a second to get his balance and walked away stiffly.

'It's either the hearing or the memory, or both,' she said. 'Are you visiting someone?'

'My name is Ruedi Lappert, and I have an appointment with Margrit Brändli in' – he looked at his watch – 'five minutes. Can you tell me where to find her?'

'Of course. I'm Nadja Rumo, activities. In quite a rush really, but I'll show you the way.'

She ploughed through double doors into a corridor. 'So you're not family,' she said over her shoulder.

'No, it's a professional matter,' Ruedi said.

'She's as sharp as a tack, I can tell you that. Here we are, room 112. The rooms on this corridor are a nice size. Now I have to get a bucket of water – the pig got overheated on the drive. Honestly, all this hassle is making me reconsider the whole farm programme.'

'Thank you,' said Ruedi to her departing back. So the old man hadn't been raving.

He knocked and entered to find Mrs Brändli sitting in an armchair. The room was spacious, as the nurse, or whoever she was, had said, and plain, with the décor all in muted tones. There was one photograph on a narrow desk of a man in holiday clothes. Apart from that, the only personal touch was a painting of a silhouette looking out on a chaotic sky. The painting faced the bed, as did Mrs Brändli's chair.

She looked him up and down. From his work on the trains, Ruedi was used to reading people on the briefest of impressions. He could fairly accurately sense how intelligent and, more importantly in his line of work, how polite a person was going to be before they opened their mouths, if they opened their mouths. Plenty of passengers had engaged with him without uttering a word. If this woman had been a passenger, he would have handled her with care and impeccable courtesy. She seemed like a person who would not take any nonsense. Direct and allergic to insincerity. And she shrank from human connection – he could feel that, too.

4

Margrit

Margrit straightened the rug across her lap and surveyed the man from Depart. You saw undertakers floating around the home on a regular basis with their bowed heads and clasped hands; the clientele kept them occupied. That's almost what she had been expecting – a black suit, sloping shoulders, the deliberate suppression of any signs of vitality. But this man Lappert was quite different. He was short, for one thing, wearing a blouson jacket in dark green with mud-coloured trousers. His shoes were bulky, creating an oddly childlike effect. He tugged gently at the right cuff of his jacket as he introduced himself, then put his hand on his heart and nodded, clicking his soft heels together, an odd mix between Austrian and Muslim manners. One of the better outcomes of Covid, she felt, was being freed from shaking hands with or kissing every damn person who passed by. He was the kind of man who might have come to her home to lay a carpet or fix the dishwasher. Unthreatening, uninteresting. Margrit pushed down a surge of irritation that bubbled up in her chest. That it had come to this!

'May I?' He gestured towards the free chair.

She knew she seemed haughty, but what she really felt was uncomfortable. Where does one start? He looked foolish sitting there with his bag on his knees, like the new boy in school. She would let him take the lead.

Mr Lappert looked around the room, and his gaze stopped at Matthias's painting, the only one she had liked well enough to keep.

It depicted a man in silhouette looking out of a window at a stormy sky. He had started it at a clinic, one of his therapies. The image was clichéd perhaps, naïve art, but something of the man's torment came through in his defeated posture, in the cruel streaks across the sky. Matthias had finished it in his grandparents' house. Not the first time he went there after a cure. Not the last time either.

'Your room is very cosy,' he said.

She thanked him brusquely. When would he get down to business?

'And how long have you lived in Sonnmatt?'

'A year and a half. So I've beaten the average.'

'The average?'

'For survival. Never mind. What is the protocol for this meeting? Do you need me to sign anything?'

'Let's see. I can tell you what we need to cover. I have a list of questions and one or two documents for you to look at. But if you don't mind, I'll introduce myself briefly. And I'd like to know a little bit more about you. Would you like me to fetch a tea or anything?'

'No tea, nothing, thank you.' An ache was building above Margrit's left eye. Always tea – you could get sick of tea. The pain was just a weak echo of the migraines she used to have when she was young. The old needle didn't scare her now; it had been blunted by age and the competition of a host of other random aches and pains. Her migraines, which had only started after Peter's birth, had been operatic. Each one had felt like a near-death experience from which she emerged diminished but glad to be alive.

The man cleared his throat. 'I suppose you could call me Bernese. I grew up in a couple of different places, finished school in Wilderswil. I still like to visit there. I spent my working life with the SBB, most of the time on the trains but also in various stations. My wife died two years ago, and I live in an apartment in Spiegel bei Bern. I have one daughter, Alessandra, and one grandson. I joined Depart myself before Maria, my wife, died.

And then I read an article about the facilitators and decided to train for this role.'

He was waiting for her to respond. A train conductor. Margrit felt her eye twitch. *Just be nice*, she thought. She had been nice so often with so many people in her life. People who did not deserve her accommodations. Did he say he lost his wife?

'I'm sorry to hear about your wife.'

His smile was unexpected. 'Thank you. It's a small thing but I still feel proud when I hear that – your wife. I miss hearing it and saying it.'

'My husband...' She paused to make room for a feeling, but nothing came. 'He died in the last century. Can you believe that? It's been a long wait since then.'

'I'm sorry for your loss.'

'Well, thank you. But when I see older couples out and about together, I never feel I would swap places with them. People think they're happy, but it's so rarely shared, don't you think? Always one paying the price for the other's happiness, and that is supposed to be enough to go round.'

He looked disconcerted. Still holding his silly bag. She should stop making pronouncements. This was the problem with not having anyone to talk to. She couldn't remember the last time she'd had an honest conversation with anyone. It was all niceties, or passive-aggressive battles. Well, he was the wrong person to talk to. Wrong person, wrong time, wrong place. Did she have to force him to get down to business?

'Don't you have questions for me – concrete questions?'

He extracted a file from his bag and laid it on the floor – at last! The bag slipped flat on the floor and he fussed with it for a minute, trying to get it to stay leaning. If he kept this up, he might irritate her to death and save himself some trouble.

'Of course. First some routine questions that I have to ask each time we meet.' She made an impatient beckoning gesture with both hands. 'So, do you stand by your wish to end your life through assisted dying with Depart?'

'I do.'

'Have your reasons changed at all?'

'If anything, they have got stronger.'

'And has there been any change in your medical circumstances?'

She shook her head. He took a stapled sheaf out of a plastic folder. 'This is the medical report written by your general practitioner. And here is the report written by the psychiatrist after the interview you had last month. He also spoke to your caseworker and the director here in Sonnmatt. It is your right to read them both. Would you like to do that?'

Nonchalant was the only way to go, the only way she would get through this. Margrit took the documents in a businesslike way. What did the situation remind her of? The time they bought the land to build their house, the notary who delayed everything by telling them a boring story about his newly discovered allergies. Nobody wants to hear about your allergies ever. Why did people not understand that? The time they were told the bad news about Frederic in the oncologist's office. That involved some charts and diagrams. The shapes had swum in front of her eyes. Not today!

Margrit did not need reading glasses. It was about the only thing that wasn't wrong with her. She scanned the doctor's typed list of infirmities. Not a pretty picture but not a tragedy by any means. Others had it worse, a lot worse, and they clung and clung. She knew that and had made her peace with it. You could even say it had made her more determined.

The psychiatrist's report was a page and a half, closely typed. Phrases assaulted her eyes. *Initially uncooperative. Depressive but not clinically depressed. Mrs Brändli has a negative worldview. Posture and body language hostile. Speaks dismissively of her sons. Resistant to socialisation. Scornful of other residents.*

'I am not scornful. Half the people here are cuckoo. I feel sorry for them, but I can't make friends with them, that's all!'

'Please, you don't have to explain. I understand that group living is not for everyone. It can be oppressive for some people.'

'If I'm scornful of anyone, it's him! Psychiatrists sit back on their comfortable chairs in their comfortable lives, and they understand nothing. All they can do is reach for a label. As if there is a formula for every kind of human suffering. As if we were computers or something! We should be sent to philosophers and poets – not damned psychiatrists. They did more harm to my Matthias than any drug dealer. Denying him help when he needed it, forcing help on him when he didn't.'

Mr Lappert was looking at Matthias's painting again as if he was trying to work something out. A simple soul, he probably thought he'd figured out something significant.

'Matthias – that's your son? I would like to speak to both your sons sooner rather than later.'

'My dear man, you can do whatever you please. You can speak to the Pope if you want to, and I'll sign whatever you bring along. Let's just get the job done.'

5

Ruedi

Ruedi walked past the cluster of daytime drinkers at the entrance of the station, some of whom he recognised from the years when this had been his base for criss-crossing the whole of Switzerland. The enormous glass roof of the station square stretched out in front of him, protecting the masses from the whims of the weather. Should we be protected from every inconvenience of life, he wondered? Even death?

Carmen was already settled at a good table in the back room of the Generationenhaus café by the time he arrived. The space was sometimes used for functions, and she had bagged two sofas facing each other on the low stage. He zig-zagged through the crowded café of mostly women, refuelling before late shopping. How relieved he was that Carmen had suggested this debriefing. He needed her solid good sense now more than ever.

She was dressed in a dark grey top with a cowl neck that gave her a medieval air. Carmen would have made a good abbess, he thought. Ruedi was used to the lack of decoration on her person: no necklace, not a single ring, not even a watch. Working in prisons, she'd got out of the habit of wearing jewellery because it could be pulled in a physical altercation. Like sugar in tea, she'd told him: give it up one day, and soon enough you won't miss it.

He moved Carmen's jacket to the side and she waited for him to get settled. He was the one with the big news. But where to start?

'She didn't like me.'

Carmen raised one eyebrow. 'Hard to credit. Go on.'

'Well, I don't think she likes anyone these days. I'm not taking it personally.'

'Good!'

A young waitress materialised next to their table. Her hair was shaved at the side but long on top, a look he felt sure Maria would have objected to. But the child was so beautiful she could have done anything with her hair and she'd still be perfect. She wrote down their coffee order – the full words. To Ruedi, she looked like a kid playing restaurants.

'Did the home director sit in?'

'No, Mrs Brändli refused to give her blessing to that. Which is a pity because we need the man on our side if we're going to do the final day on the premises.'

'And is the client willing to go to the Depart location if needed?'

'She's very dry about it. "I'll do it on the top of the Schilthorn if that's what it takes," was what she said. Made herself laugh at that one.'

'Sounds like she was relaxed with you.'

'I don't know. I wasn't quite up to her standards. I suppose she comes from one of those noble Bernese families or whatever. But she's so old and infirm, she doesn't give a damn anymore. Definitely doesn't suffer fools gladly. I think she saw me as an irritation.'

'So she didn't open up?'

The coffees arrived, and they paused their conversation to watch the girl benignly. She wouldn't last long in the job serving at that pace. Ruedi could see that Carmen was having the same thought.

'Sweet,' she said when the girl had moved on.

'Yes, sweet.' It was hard to imagine that Margrit Brändli had ever been sweet or lovely but she had probably had her burst of beauty like every other young person. Ruedi didn't think anyone came of age without having this moment of youthful glory. Alessandra's turn came around in her early twenties when she met Florian's father.

'Did you find her interesting? What else did she say?'

'She didn't really open up. Mentioned at one point that one of her sons had been a drug addict. But indirectly. She just wants things to be businesslike.'

'Is that so?' Carmen suddenly seemed to have tuned out of the conversation, looking at the plant between them.

'How was your day, Carmen?'

With an effort, she came back to him. 'You mentioning drugs. It made me think about one of our inmates who was a mule. I know the drugs do terrible damage, but these women, they are so clueless. And the sentences are harsh. Years without seeing their kids, and with nothing to send home for their keep. This woman today, it was her daughter's First Communion day. She cried the whole day, I was told. I was too busy to visit the block and I can tell you, I was glad not to have to see her.'

'That is tough.'

'It's no wonder I'm drawn to the Depart clients and their bid for freedom. The ultimate freedom.'

Carmen had many theories about the people who came to Depart. It was one of her favourite subjects. After years of superficial interactions with the people in his life, Ruedi enjoyed these forays into philosophical conversation. Even Maria would not face up to any hard truths. Part of her strategy to deal with illness was not to give it airtime. As if that would rob MS of any of its power.

'Remember when you talked about courage the last time we were here?' Ruedi said. 'I think it might be closer to stubbornness. But one thing these people have in common is that they are interesting.'

'It's like that line from *Anna Karenina*. All happy families are the same but all unhappy families are different in their unhappiness.

Something like that. All our clients are different, because they are refusing to take the natural path.'

Anna Karenina! Ruedi had become a bit of a reader from being stuck on long journeys, but never anything like that. Had Alessandra read the classics? He had no idea. Would his grandson Florian ever come across books like that? He was good at school, and Ruedi liked the idea of him studying at university one day.

Ruedi did not feel qualified to say anything about Carmen's comment. But it was quite an idea. And it made him wonder if he and Maria had managed to create a happy family or been unhappy in a unique way. Whatever unhappiness they endured came from the outside, though, not from them.

'Speaking of families,' he said, 'I'm minding my grandson this evening, and I need to go home first to get rid of all this stuff.'

'I'm getting this,' she said, swiping the bill from under the little plant pot. 'Off you go. I need to phone my mother anyway. Congratulations on today. And don't forget, you can call me any time. Did you offer her a notebook, by the way?'

'No. Do you think I should?'

'Worth a try. Send me over that girl on your way out.'

*

Alessandra and Florian lived in a converted old townhouse with a glass atrium connecting it to an identical building across what had once been a laneway. Inside, on either side of the stairwell, the kitchens of each apartment faced each other, fully on view through floor-to-ceiling windows. Anyone walking up the stairs could see in and observe the same kitchen layout and two families on each floor doing the same things across from each other. Ruedi didn't know how Alessandra could stand it. The rest of the apartment was in the original building, thankfully normal, hidden behind doors and walls.

He took the lift to the second floor. As soon as the doors opened, Ruedi saw Florian, head bent over his books at the kitchen table. Florian was incapable of sitting properly on a chair. He always had a knee up or a leg tucked under him, like some kind of water bird.

Florian noticed his grandfather on the landing and came to open the door. His welcoming smile was more polite than glad. Ruedi left his shoes inside the door and followed the boy into the kitchen, which was filled with soft evening light from the atrium. All the units were stainless steel, and the table looked like it had been rescued from a skip. Despite the utilitarian design and the missing wall, Alessandra had managed to make the place homely and a little chaotic, with coloured pots and containers squeezed in everywhere and Florian's artwork on every upright surface. One end of the kitchen table was taken up with a row of plants at different stages of growth.

'How are the avocados getting on?' Ruedi asked.

'Great. This one is two weeks old, just potted. I nearly gave up on it. These ones are all a month apart. We've moved the big ones to the shower room now.'

'Any more in the pipeline?'

'No, Mami said we should take a break.'

'Fair enough.'

But Florian didn't look like he agreed. He closed his maths book with a sigh.

'Homework done?' said Ruedi.

'I've done enough. Mami said we could have *café complet*.'

While Florian set the table, Ruedi went to the fridge and took out cheese, ham, garlic sausage, yoghurts, olives and tomatoes. A paper bag of bread rolls sat next to the sink. Alessandra was well organised; he respected that.

The meal began in silence. Florian had always been a chatty child, and there had never been any need to think of topics to talk about, but over the past year, self-consciousness had found him, and the bubbliness had disappeared. Ruedi supposed it was good that he was no longer in his own little world, but it made him harder company. He had left the football team too; that had been a good topic. But Ruedi didn't ask him about hobbies anymore, because he seemed to drop out of everything he started. Something Alessandra should have been firmer about. She was allowing him to be flighty.

'Did Mami tell you about my school project?'

'The avocados?'

'That's not for school, that's for me.'

'Oh.'

'My school project is about grandparents. We have to pick a grandparent and interview them.'

'Really? What kind of interview?'

'About your life.'

'Oh. That doesn't really sound like my sort of thing. What if you don't have grandparents?'

'But I do. And my other grandparents don't speak German. So it's only you, really.'

'Aren't you going to eat any cheese?'

'I don't like cheese.'

'Don't like cheese? Well, have a yoghurt. You have to eat more than bread and ham.'

'We could do the interview now.'

'You speak Albanian, don't you? I bet it would be really interesting to hear about life in Kosovo. You could phone them.'

'You can't do it on the phone. I don't understand their accent anyway. I understand my papi and the people around here but not the old people there.'

'That sounds like an excuse to me.'

Florian looked close to tears, and Ruedi felt a distinct urge to slap the child. Not the slightest resilience. Alessandra must have known he wouldn't be happy about this interview thing. Did she trick him into being alone with Florian? He looked across the landing to the other kitchen. Two women and two little girls were sitting up very straight at the table, like characters on a stage pretending to be a model family. What did he look like facing Florian with cutlery clenched tight in his fists? An angry man with a nervous boy.

When he was that age, he had been reunited with his mother after an eight-year gap. He remembered long evenings of not knowing what to say to each other. It had almost made him miss the Sutter farm, because there no one had paid much attention to him. But the way his mother looked at him, all that sadness and need, it hurt.

He was ashamed for making Florian feel uneasy in his company. The boy stared at his plate, the ham torn into tiny pieces in his effort to avoid the veins of fat.

'How about jam?' Ruedi asked, by way of a peace offering.

Florian looked up warily, visibly trying to read his grandfather's mood.

'And when you're done, we can move into the sitting room for the interview. I don't remember everything, but I'll do my best.'

After they had tidied up, Florian led the way to the sofa, put the tablet on a cushion between them, and pressed record.

Ruedi cleared his throat. 'I was born in 1949. I suppose you want to know about my parents. My father was from Valais. He left Switzerland when I was very young and went to work in a hotel in London.'

'You don't have to talk loudly.'

'Ah, OK. Where was I? My mother worked in a hotel too. Later she worked in a factory and a hospital. She was mostly a cleaner. We lived in Wilderswil for a few years and moved to Bern when I was fourteen. I did my apprenticeship in a printers – I'm a trained printer. But I didn't like the smell of the ink. I felt sick for the first six months until I got used to it, wanted to stop every day. Don't put that in.'

'Mami said you lived in a children's home.'

'She said that. What else did she say?'

'She said it was sad.'

Ruedi pulled at his cuff. 'It was just a practical thing. My mother needed to find a better job, and so I went to stay in a home for a while. Then I went back to her.'

'How long did you live in the home?'

'A few years. I don't remember exactly.'

'A boy in my class went to a home. He was breaking things and starting fires. He was the oldest in the class.'

'I didn't do anything like that.'

'Did you try to run away?'

'There was nowhere to go. Look, Florian, it wasn't that bad, and it wasn't that exciting. We had enough to eat, normal clothes, some toys. I had friends. Some of us missed our parents, our families; some didn't, either because they couldn't remember them or because their homes weren't that great. Not everyone has a nice place like this with good people around, you know.'

'Who was your best friend?'

'My best friend was Dänu. We met when we were eight. He and I were the only ones who weren't Catholic, so we were often thrown together. Dänu had been taken in by a family, but they sent him back because he couldn't do maths.'

'Because of maths! I'm not good at maths.'

'With Dänu, it was extreme. He couldn't make head nor tail of maths, even simple sums, and the family only discovered this after he started school. The teacher said he was a hopeless case, would never understand the basics. And the whole reason the family got him was because it was a house of girls and the father was a carpenter. He wanted a boy to grow up with the business, learn alongside him. They were sorry to send him back, but they couldn't keep a child who wouldn't be of use.'

'But that's so mean.'

'They continued to invite him for Christmas and things like that. The girls were so fond of him. He had been three years with the family, and it wasn't that easy to settle back in the home because no one remembered him. But he became my friend.'

'Is he still your friend?'

'No, it was so long ago.'

Dänu died of some childhood illness. There had never been any explanation. He was sick, he went to hospital, and he never came back. Ruedi could still picture him exactly, even though he hadn't had a photo to keep or anything to remind him of Dänu all these years. After he had gone, Ruedi didn't mind leaving the home so much. It wasn't the same anymore without his friend. He didn't really care what happened to himself.

'Why don't I tell you about meeting your grandmother?' He pointed to the screen, encouraging Florian to keep going. He wanted to get him over this maudlin stuff. There were good years to talk about too. 'Maria's sister was in my class at vocational college, did you know that? She was the only girl printer apprentice in the whole school. Everyone thought her parents must be mad. Well, we hardly spoke back then, because she kept to herself. But later, a couple of years after finishing, I saw her at a dance in the Mahogany Hall. She was with a very pretty girl, and I worked up the courage to go over and say hello to them both. Renata introduced me to her sister Maria. She was wearing a green minidress, and I asked her to dance. I walked them both home, and I soon became part of the family. I was there constantly. Within a few months, I could understand Italian, or at least their dialect. They were very impressed with that. Nice people.'

They heard the key in the door.

'Then we got married, your mother came along, and we all lived happily ever after. The End. That's plenty, isn't it? See if your mami needs any help.'

As he heard the two of them greeting each other on the other side of the door, he breathed a sigh of relief. Why did Alessandra have to tell him about the home? The main thing was that he would never betray his mother's secrets, the things she'd shared with him and the things she hadn't wanted him to know about. He had never even told Maria, and certainly not Alessandra. That was as it should be.

6

Margrit

Margrit picked at her supper. She'd eaten the gherkins but wasn't really in the mood for cold cuts. The last meal she'd prepared herself had been seventeen months previously, before she'd been admitted to Sonnmatt. If Nadja had ever suggested it, she wouldn't have minded access to the kitchen to lend a hand now and then. But no, it was all black-and-white films and stretching exercises in this place. Frederic would not have fitted in either.

Frederic. She missed his eyes, his expressive hands, his way of walking. Twenty-three years on, it was the physicality of her husband she missed the most.

She was aware that, early on, she had decided to remember her marriage in a certain way. People are so sympathetic to a widow, and she really wanted to deserve that, so she chose to see the deceased Frederic in the warmest possible light. And there were good things about him. He was not mean with money. When you didn't earn your own, that became very important. It wasn't his style to check with her where every penny went; he didn't raise his eyebrows or make remarks when she bought something for herself. He was not overly forceful with his opinions, rehearsing them on her, as many husbands did. They hardly even talked about the vote in '71, though she was sure he had voted yes to female suffrage. He didn't drink too much, for those times, and his temper never made her afraid. All negative statements, flaws he lacked. Could she only commend him for what he was not? Never mind: the point was he was a good man.

When he died, she packed away her complaints, his reliance on her servitude, his inability to truly see her, his dullness and lack of passion – those sorts of things. She packed them away and praised him in his absence to anyone who prompted. Hard-working, a good provider, that went without saying. He kept up his end of the deal on that front.

She had come to the conclusion that for men, the value of the wife lies in her ability to serve and to submit, to put the needs of the family above her own. That way, the man can thrive, whether he's the man leading the country or the man driving the train.

Regardless of how determined Margrit was to be different or 'modern', as she used to think of herself, once she got together with Frederic there was only one possible outcome. She wasn't convinced that women would ever escape this, despite the vote and things like that, because the essential does not change.

Margrit used to look at her mother and feel sorry for her. The way Vreni dressed, the things she said. How limited her life was. Not only pity – Margrit also felt a little scorn. How could she let herself get like that? Ha, well now she knew. True, Margrit had had nicer clothes, a nicer home and more square kilometres to roam, but she had also ended up playing a supporting role in life under someone else's name. Margrit couldn't work after she was visibly pregnant; that was the general consensus between her doctor, her husband and her employer. From then on she was needed in the home, and she gave herself up to all that. It was, after all, a well-worn path, the very definition of good fortune.

And now she was pursued by this bitterness she had pushed out of sight for so long. It had risen up and come hunting down the years to find her. That was another thing she wanted to escape – the ruminations, the reckonings. She'd had enough.

She was not only escaping. She was also reaching for something. Not freedom necessarily, not oblivion, but the feeling of putting herself first. She wanted to own herself once and for all, regardless of what the others – her husband, her children, the experts, even the people in this home – might think or want.

Margrit speared a pickled onion and popped it in her mouth. Now *that* was bitter.

7

Ruedi

Ruedi usually found whatever stationery he needed in the big Migros on Marktgasse. Black biros, a block of paper, Sellotape – that kind of thing. He knew where the Stauffacher *papeterie* was, but he had never crossed the threshold until today. Thanks to Carmen, he was forced to enter this decidedly female territory.

He walked a few steps and halted in the middle of the central aisle, radiating confusion, or so he felt. There was a bank of greeting cards to his left, rows of coloured pens to his right, letter-writing sets, magnets, wrapping paper, pencil cases, paints, markers, coloured paper, teddies, gift books. Absolutely anything you could imagine – except for notebooks, which were frustratingly not visible. Much as he needed help, he was dreading the inevitable ambush by a shop assistant. His usual rule was not to go into a shop where the staff would approach you.

A kind-looking woman dressed like a chic pastor intercepted him in front of the calendars. 'Good day. Can I help you with something?'

'I'm looking for a notebook.' At least he had his request ready.

'What kind of notebook?'

He mimed the size he had in mind.

'A school notebook, softback, hardback, lined, blank, or a planner?'

'For writing,' he said.

'Ah, just writing. This way, please. We have a selection of hardback notebooks over here.'

She left him in an aisle of diaries and notebooks in an unending array of colours and designs. They were adorned with images of tropical beaches, foliage, cartoon characters, abstract designs – he could hardly take it all in. His eye was drawn to a free-standing display of elastic-bound classic-looking notebooks in different colours, but he almost dropped one when he turned it over to check the price. Carmen hadn't warned him about that. He turned back to the main selection. Recipe notebooks, travel notebooks, to-do lists, gardening notebooks – everything seemed to be for a special purpose. He started to feel warm despite the air conditioning.

After picking up and putting down at least a dozen that looked to be the right size, albeit with garish covers, he worked his way over to the lower corner, where the most basic lined hardback notebooks, probably the plainest things in the shop, were modestly waiting for a charitable glance. One of these would do. It took an inordinate length of time to decide between navy, forest green and burgundy. Black wouldn't do. In the end he chose a green one and went to the till.

A different woman served him. She looked young and bright, and he could imagine she had a room full of these colourful, optimistic products at home. She reminded him a tiny bit of a young Alessandra – the same little acrobat's body and languorous eyes – and he felt a gentle rumble of remorse at some of his critical thoughts about his daughter recently. He, of all people, should be sympathetic to a woman trying a raise a son on her own. With the notebook tucked under his arm in a paper bag, he made his way back through the safer main bookshop to the exit, feeling relieved and not a little proud.

On his way home by bus, he rehearsed his explanation for the notebook, as coached by Carmen. *We have found it can be helpful at this time to write down some of your thoughts. Here is a sheet of prompt writings – no, writing prompts – to guide you.*

Only if you feel like it. Many people find it helpful. Damn, he was repeating himself. He sensed a pulse of curiosity around him, but when he looked up, he couldn't catch anyone staring. Suddenly self-conscious, he wasn't sure if his lips were moving or not, so he stopped. It would be fine. Knowing Mrs Brändli, she wouldn't listen to him anyway.

The bus passed a café where he'd once had a debriefing with Carmen. He remembered her saying she was in awe of death and in awe of those who invited death in. That's what had drawn her to the work.

'I guess prison wasn't extreme enough for me,' she'd said.

'I'm not a person of extremes, and I am also drawn to the work,' he pointed out gently. 'You could also see it as a form of service?'

'I appreciate you framing it that way.'

Earlier that day, he had accompanied Carmen to the home of a lawyer with stage four cancer. The police had arrived quickly, and Carmen had completed the paperwork and handed over to the undertakers in time for them to have a coffee together nearby before taking their separate buses. He remembered their conversation clearly.

'The poor man was in a bad way. It was urgent, merciful. The most urgent I've seen since I started,' Carmen said, keeping her voice steady. 'You'll find that the cases vary a lot. Sometimes the client's situation is not objectively unbearable. Or does it even make sense to speak of thresholds of what is bearable when it is in essence a subjective concept? I can't bear my neighbour practising the clarinet, for instance. What can't you bear?'

'Fare dodgers. No, it's true – we all bear things that we can't bear.' Ruedi automatically thought of Maria's trials, so much worse than his.

'For most of our clients, death is not imminent but on the horizon. They are people with a strong sense of personal dignity.

But they also have a need to be in control. The two things are not unrelated. I hesitate to use the word proud, but they find it harder than most to be helpless. I do think they have courage – and they need a certain kind of help: our help. The courage is compelling. Overall, I find them straightforward enough to deal with. They have things figured out. It's the family you have to watch out for.'

A recorded voice announced his stop and Ruedi got off the bus, suddenly preoccupied about his meeting with Mrs Brändli's sons the next day.

8

Margrit

A lull hung over the home today. This was how it always was for at least a day after a death. Margrit had been woken long after midnight by the sound of a woman crying. Not a young woman, yet her crying was as plaintive as a child's. That's what Margrit heard first in her dream, a child crying 'Mami, Mami'. She was back in Mendenswil trying the doors upstairs, looking for her baby brother so she could comfort him, but the doors were sealed shut. By the time she fully woke, the crying voice was being hushed by a louder male voice. She preferred the crying to the hushing. Then both voices died away and there was only the sound of efficient footsteps.

In the morning, she found out that Mrs Schwab had died in the night – the one who went around asking everyone for her car keys. There had been complaints and talk of transferring her to the secure wing. That wouldn't happen now.

Margrit had lunch in her room and, when everything was cleared away, took out the accordion folder where she kept her paperwork. She opened up her last tax return and checked that she had the latest statement for each of the accounts listed. It reminded her of her working days. She had been proud to be good with numbers and not only a typist. Her mother had been right to push her towards the bookkeeping qualification. Had she ever acknowledged that? From farm girl to shop girl to office girl. She was glad she'd given her mother something to boast about.

Her phone lit up and she saw Peter's name on the screen. A text message. Margrit cleared her papers away before reading it. One thing at a time. Peter would appreciate the pains she was taking, soon.

He wanted to visit on Saturday, with Matthias. What time would suit her? Well, this was new – her sons' first ever joint visit. She supposed it was to be expected. At least Peter hadn't asked to come with Nathalie.

If only she could have warmed to her daughter-in-law. There had been a phase when Nathalie had seemed like a good choice for Peter. She fitted with his need to aim high. With her perfect teeth and elegant clothes, she definitely made a good first impression. Nathalie believed in using her free time productively. Suddenly Peter's diary was full with a multitude of day trips and once-in-a-lifetime experiences. She was the kind of person that would drag you up a mountain for fondue in an igloo one weekend and to the opera in Vienna the next. She made photo books. There had been a trip to Dubai, a proposal on the banks of the Seine. She managed to make Peter look like a romantic. Peter confided in Margrit that Nathalie's childhood had been chaotic and that he felt it his destiny to give her stability and happiness. Though it looked like he was taking on a demanding job, Margrit was pleased for him.

But you could see there was something forced about Nathalie, a brittle edge to her brightness. When Margrit visited their first shared apartment, it was Nathalie who gave Margrit the tour and explained about the theme and colour scheme, her pet pieces of furniture. It was like a Pfister showroom. Peter had told her Nathalie didn't want to merge their possessions when they moved in together – she wanted a clean slate. She had saved up for this eventuality, expecting him to match the amount.

In the bedroom hung three large black-and-white photographs of Nathalie in seductive poses wearing lingerie or less. Peter had gifted her a studio photoshoot as a present for her thirtieth, she explained. No doubt he had his instructions, Margrit thought. She understood then why he had made himself scarce, choosing that moment to fetch a vase for her flowers. Nathalie showed no sign of awkwardness, explaining how the photographer had put her at her ease and kept everything tasteful. Oh, but Margrit would have been glad to miss out on this insight into their lives.

'I'll skip the en-suite,' she said. 'I can see the tiles from here. Very nice. Maybe Peter needs a hand.'

She found her son plumping up the bouquet at the kitchen table. He opened the cupboard under the sink, swiped the cut stalks into a small green bin, wiped up the drops on the counter and replaced the pristine cloth inside the cupboard in a special container with sections for cloths, brushes and washing-up liquid. Margrit watched the procedure with interest. The kitchen was returned to its untouched state. We all want things to be different and better when we start out. She couldn't blame them for trying.

Margrit wondered in those days how Nathalie would deal with the disruption of children. Her own way, for sure. But it took them several years to start a family, and Margrit sensed the delay was a worry for them. She was careful never to make Nathalie feel like she was waiting. She hoped good news would come one day, and it did. Looking back, that period before the children were born was the time when she could have cultivated a friendship with her daughter-in-law. But they didn't seek each other out, and Margrit sensed that Nathalie wouldn't relax around her until she was a mother herself.

During those years of waiting, the couple once took her out to lunch on Mother's Day. It might have been the year Frederic died. As they left the restaurant, a waitress stood at the door offering a rose to the departing mothers. Margrit took her rose automatically, too slow to realise that she might need to save Nathalie.

She looked back to smile at Peter and saw Nathalie's face, briefly stricken, as she held up a hand to the girl in refusal.

Nathalie managed her pregnancies and infants by the book. As soon as Meret took her first steps and started to show her own will, Nathalie went into training mode. The same for Luna. She kept her daughters subdued with words – a torrent of words. She talked to them like a domineering nurse addressing patients on a psychiatric ward, which appeared to be how she viewed her tiny tots. Every decision was signalled in advance, everything explained and justified at length. Nothing was negotiable. Her running commentary on their behaviour and movements kept the children corralled at all times. To Margrit's dismay, she fast-tracked them out of toddlerhood and did not enjoy high spirits or silliness.

Unfortunately, the little girls brought out high spirits and silliness in Margrit. She liked to dance with them, tickle them, make up funny words. It was as if a new, more natural mother had belatedly woken up in her.

Meanwhile, Nathalie was vigilant for signs of ADHD or Asperger's and this was a frequent topic of discussion when they saw each other. Margrit refused to believe there was anything out of the ordinary about the girls. So what if Meret was anxious about getting her hands dirty, or if Luna walked on her tiptoes. Children were meant to be eccentric! When Nathalie started diagnosing her own husband and his brother with this and that, Margrit would leave the room. The woman worked in marketing, not medicine.

On one visit – the girls must have been three or four years old, just fifteen months between them – Nathalie was ready to go but Margrit wanted to give the children a quick *zvieri* before the long drive home. While they ate their bread and honey and slices of apple, she made up a story about a caterpillar driving a bus where all the passengers were insects. As she added each new passenger, the girls roared with laughter and it became a little bit unruly.

Luna spilled her juice and Nathalie called a halt to the whole thing, wiping the girls' hands and faces with a cloth.

While the women cleared the table together – to Margrit's exasperation, Nathalie never let her tidy up her own kitchen – the children ran upstairs and hid. Margrit left Nathalie to load the dishwasher.

'Caterpillar is coming to find you,' she called up the stairs and heard shrieks from one of the front bedrooms. She continued in that vein until Nathalie emerged from the kitchen. Her face was blotchy and there were crumbs in her hair. For years, they had made do with sighs and body language to express their annoyance; Margrit sensed this was about to change.

'Meret, Luna! Get down here,' Nathalie barked, and turned to her mother-in-law. 'Maybe next time you will let us leave at the time that suits us as a family.'

'I only wanted them to have a little snack. Luna said she was hungry.'

'Peter,' Nathalie called, 'can you go and find them, please? Peter! Where is he? Is he hiding too? Unbelievable!' Nathalie went back into the kitchen and Margrit watched through the door as she wiped the table in angry arcs.

Margrit wanted to make amends. She went in and wrapped the rest of the loaf of bread in a tea towel. 'This *Zopf* is homemade. You can take the rest home if you like.'

'I have enough bread at home, thank you.' Nathalie cast her eyes up to the lamp over the table, as if seeking an answer to something. She nodded to herself and continued: 'Margrit, do I need to explain? Your little snack will put them off their dinner. It means they're more likely to fall asleep on the journey. It means I won't have time to get the things done that I wanted to do before work tomorrow.'

'That's a lot of fuss for an extra half an hour.' Those minutes meant so much to Margrit. She wouldn't see the girls again for weeks.

'We planned to leave at three. I mentioned that when I arrived. It's past four o'clock now.'

'I know routine is important to you. I was more flexible with the boys.'

'Flexible? More like indifferent, from what Peter has told me. Girls, come down right now!'

It was Margrit's turn to have a blotchy face. She stared at Nathalie until her daughter-in-law turned away.

Peter was in the garden. If Nathalie had listened to him, she would know that. He had said he wanted to take some cuttings with him.

Margrit went upstairs to her room. She remembered thinking: *Let them find their own children and their own way out.*

When she talked to Peter about the tensions in those early years, he pleaded with her not to create a rift.

'But I'm not creating a rift! I'm just being myself.'

'Then don't be yourself,' was his advice. 'Put the girls first and act nice.'

So Margrit smoothed things over and kept up the contact for the girls' sake, even when Peter moved to the far side of Zurich and it was more of an effort. She wanted to know them, to watch them grow, hopefully to mean something to them. Yet, despite her efforts, they relaxed less around her as the years went by. Perhaps her visits were not frequent enough. They would welcome her warmly, almost as a reflex, but soon drifted away to another part of the house, leaving the adults to labour through the visit together. For Margrit, it was like a repeat of what had happened with the boys. They did not progress past their familial roles into a genuine relationship.

Margrit stayed in her room until the undertakers for Mrs Schwab had been and gone. It wasn't like her to be cowardly, but she didn't want to risk seeing the faces of the men who would soon come for her. She was afraid she might read some knowledge in their eyes that would open the door to fear. Be not afraid – that was one piece of advice she was prepared to take from the Bible.

9

Ruedi

'I'll be perfectly honest with you – I broke something in my mother.'

Matthias turned his head to the side and pulled at his ponytail. He looked around at the handful of customers in the Sonnmatt café, taking them in one by one. 'I'd be better off visiting one of these sweet people. Maybe the old biddy with the fake flowers tied to her Zimmer frame. Yes, I'll take her.'

Ruedi glanced at his watch. He wasn't sure how much more he could take. The man was in his late fifties, and he sounded like an adolescent.

Matthias removed the sugar packs from the square bowl and started shuffling them. 'The thing is, I've been functional for years, but she won't see it. She looks at me and sees disaster, betrayal. She was so sure for so long that she would bury me, and that made her furious. I don't think the anger ever subsided.'

'Well, I suppose what I'm getting at is whether you feel able to support your mother in this course of action, whether you will be there for her. As in, literally, on the day.'

'We don't have a date yet, do we? Good God. Peter wants us to have lunch beforehand. Did you ever hear anything more ridiculous? It's borderline outrageous. The three of us haven't had lunch together for years, decades even. In fact, it was never a thing we did. He probably only wants me there as a distraction. Peter isn't the best conversationalist in the world, you know. Or you're about to find out. Let me tell you about Peter.'

Ruedi looked around to check if there was any sign of another Brändli. Peter was due to arrive any minute. 'Look, I think it's better if we just stick to the matter at hand. As I understand it, you have no concerns about your mother not being of sound mind. You don't think she's under pressure from anyone, including yourself.'

'I'm going to say something that you will possibly not understand, but you would if you had walked in my shoes. I'm fifty-nine. I am ready for my sonhood to be over. If that's not a word, I don't care. I've been a son for way too long, and the burden nearly killed me. I'm out.'

The coffee tasted nasty, one of those times when you wonder if the whole coffee business is a massive marketing con. Somebody, somewhere was laughing all the way to the bank after convincing the world that coffee beans were a good basis for a drink.

'I'll tell you what I miss.' Matthias was now lining the sachets of sugar into a row. 'Being able to have a damn cigarette indoors like a civilised person. Being able to have a drink and a cigarette at the same time, while sitting down, while warm and dry. It's a mean thing to have taken away.'

Ruedi couldn't remember what he'd asked the man. He checked his papers. 'Would you mind writing down your address here? I have your number, and I'll text you when the date is confirmed anyway. This is for the paperwork afterwards.'

Matthias's sunken cheeks were dark shadows on his face. He must be one of the few ex-heroin addicts of his generation who'd made it this far. Ruedi wondered what had got him through. It couldn't all be raw luck. His family had probably moved mountains for him.

'You're looking at me in a judgemental way – I know that look. I already told you, Peter is the man for the paperwork.' He shuddered. 'This crappy canteen, that smell. It reminds me of rehab places I've stayed at. They must have the same damn cookbook in every institution in Switzerland.'

'Yes, well. You must have had a nice upbringing.'

'I have to laugh. The way she goes on about my father... she's convinced herself it was a real love story. Au con-fucking-traire.'

'They were married a long time. I suppose she prefers to remember the good years. Most marriages do have them.'

'Maybe so, but the atmosphere was not so jolly when we were growing up. Ask Peter.'

'Mr Brändli, you seem to think that I have come to pass judgement on your mother or your family. That's not the case. I am only here to help make this process, this decision of your mother's, as trouble-free as possible.'

'I have to keep an eye on the time. Got to catch a bus to Mendenswil – the other end of the canton. Where is Peter? He's the one who wanted us to see her together.'

'Mendenswil – you know people there?'

'None of our people left these days, but I still like to visit the old place. The best hikes in the world are there. That's my therapy.'

'What old place?'

'The Sutter place, my grandparents' farm. That's where Mami grew up. Didn't she say?'

'She was Margrit Sutter?'

'Still is, underneath it all, I suppose.' He stood up and patted his pockets. 'Smoke break for me.'

Ruedi became aware of his weight on the chair, his feet on the ground. The world went quiet around him, and he spread his hands flat on the table. Mendenswil. A place he had last seen over sixty years ago as a child. He could see it before him now. The house on the slope, three rows of windows with shutters pinned back, the long pig shed at an angle, the field sweeping down to the river. And he could almost feel it again, the pain in his stomach as he approached on his way home from school, the feeling that he would never belong with this family. Tears held back all day, missing poor Dänu, missing kind Sister Camilla and even the grumpy cook, missing the dormitory with all its rough and tumble. In the house with all the windows the food was better and the rooms were warmer, as were the clothes. The people were not mean to him, but they did not really care to know him. The togetherness was gone forever.

And into that lake of loneliness – that awful effort to speak when spoken to, to get out of the way if not needed, to be on hand when needed, the skill of service Sister Camilla had talked about – stepped Margrit, a person who finally looked at him and saw something worth kindling. Margrit Sutter with the lovely wavy hair and smart clothes, the girl who smiled and played Ludo with him and told stories of Bern. Sledging. She took him sledging. They sat on the same sledge, and she wore a red knitted hat. There hadn't been any slopes around the children's home. No sledges either. It was all coming back, and Ruedi's heart raced and lurched as the emotions of that childhood winter tumbled into the reality of today.

He was still staring down the long tunnel of time when a heavy middle-aged man came lumbering towards him. With an effort, Ruedi responded to his outstretched hand.

'Mr Lappert? Peter Brändli. Sorry I'm late. Traffic. I just saw my brother on his way out the gate. He said he didn't visit our mother and that you'd explain.'

Ruedi gathered his thoughts and his manners. He would never have put the two men together. They didn't look like they came from the same geographical region, let alone the same family. Built like a Schwingen wrestler who had gone to seed, Peter was as dark as Matthias was fair, and much bulkier.

'Nice to meet you. Yes, your mother was asleep and your brother didn't want to disturb her. Said he'd try again next week.'

'You'd think he could have waited a few more minutes to go in with me. I've just driven two and a half hours.' Peter raised his shoulders and held out his hands in resignation.

'Would you like to try and see your mother first, or should we begin?'

'Let's talk first. I don't want to keep you waiting any longer.' He sat down opposite Ruedi. 'Look, I'm a practical person. My mother has not been happy for a long time. Her life has shrunk, and her health has been failing. Actually, this year has been good so far, but last year was her annus horribilis – a fractured collarbone from a fall, pancreatitis in September, and Covid in December. I honestly don't know how she pulled through, but she got over it all and now she's come out the other side asking for this. I don't know what to think. All the other poor bastards in here just get on with things, but Mother – well, she was always the kind of person who wasn't afraid to complain to the manager. I'm sorry, I'm being flippant. Where do I fit in? Am I supposed to do something?'

'The important thing is for me to know that you believe Mrs Brändli is doing this of her own volition – that she is not under pressure from anyone.'

'She seems very clear, very certain. But I only heard about this a little over a week ago. She told me on the phone. That's unusual, isn't it?'

'Well—'

'She's more talkative than she has been in years. Suddenly she has something to talk about. What did she say to you?'

'Similar things. I have the same impressions you have. But I am not emotionally involved. Do you mind me asking if you have someone to speak to about this? You'll need support if you're going to give support.' This was on Carmen's list of handy platitudes for all situations, and Ruedi felt insincere using her lines. He liked the man, with his frank way of expressing himself. Peter reminded him of one of Margrit's brothers, the one that was obsessed with hunting and shocked Ruedi one day by appearing around the corner of the house with a dead chamois slung over his shoulder. As if there wasn't enough killing on that farm. Peter would have made a great farmer. Instead, he probably sat behind a desk all day.

'I haven't mentioned it to anyone since I heard, not even my wife. Yes, I know it sounds weird. But I feel strangely ashamed. Like this is a sign we've let her down. People will think we abandoned her. I love her, but she's not an easy person, even without the mobility problem and the care she needs.'

'I wouldn't worry about what other people think. Everyone knows someone who's made this end-of-life choice by now. People get it.'

'Can we talk about dates? I have an important trip booked that I can't change. Ideally, I'd like to have time to sort out the basics for the funeral and the estate before I leave. Or do the whole thing afterwards; that might even be better.'

Ruedi's mouth was dry. He watched Peter call up the calendar on his phone. Margrit's words came back to him: 'They are tired of me, and I am tired of them.'

'We don't know about dates yet. I have to talk to the director here, and to the organisation. Mrs Brändli says end of the summer.'

'Yes, I know. How poetic.'

10

Margrit

Peter had given her a book. Memoirs of a woman her age who had led an exciting life. What was he trying to say? Margrit's legs were too stiff and swollen to get up. She leafed through a few pages, saw a picture of the woman on horseback and gave up. The idea of getting up on a horse now! She'd had a similar problem with her legs towards the end of pregnancy – but she couldn't remember which pregnancy. A strong wave of weariness, almost a spasm, passed through her body. If her sons were the product of her married love, what did that say about her and Frederic? Would she have had better results with someone else, maybe even Luigi? What an awful line of thought. She really shouldn't think of the two men in the same brainwave.

And how could she think of her sons as the random outcome of anything? They were real people with their own place in the world, a right to their own existence independent of the crazy woman who happened to be their mother.

Anyway, Peter and Matthias came from something good. She did love Frederic. 'I loved you, Frederic,' she said out loud, and pinched her thigh, annoyed with herself. They had enjoyed each other physically. They wanted children. It was a common goal. They hoped and planned for children and these were the ones they were given, the ones they loved.

That was the prize of marriage – to freely love at last. It was not unusual for unmarried girls to avoid going all the way when

Margrit was young. There was so much at stake. What would the boy think of you; would he want you anymore; who would he tell; what if the worst happened?

When she was working in Loeb, one of her younger cousins had come to her needing help to get an abortion, which she couldn't get in Catholic Fribourg. In Bern it wasn't that easy either. You had to know the right doctor who was willing to sign letters and make phone calls. After helping Trudi with her situation, Margrit was even more determined to avoid any trouble. But that didn't mean she didn't feel passion.

When she thought of Luigi, she remembered them glued together, in a state of constant arousal. They were never not touching, did everything they could with their hands, in doorways, on benches, but they didn't have the privacy for more. With her landlady always hanging around, her place was out of the question, and Luigi shared his small apartment with three work colleagues, including his fiancée's brother. Once, in a moment of recklessness for them both, he took her back to the apartment, but they were interrupted and agreed afterwards it was for the best. Open air was safer.

She didn't dare take him back to visit her parents. What would have been the point when he was promised to marry someone else? And she was afraid they would make some stupid remarks about Italians, which was bad enough to hear from strangers.

But she wanted to show him her part of the Swiss countryside, and so they went there once by train. She took him on a walk along the Aergera. When they came to a forest glade, not having passed anyone for ages, he pulled her out of sight of the path and asked to see her breasts in the daylight. She removed her shirt and dropped it on the moss, standing before him wearing only shorts and sensible shoes. It would have been a strange tableau for anyone to see, the Virgin Margrit with Luigi kneeling in front of her, for all the world like a devout man having a visitation.

Much as she enjoyed building up experience and feeling like a woman of the world, Margrit could never forget that Luigi had chosen someone else, and that made her keep her resolve. He tried persuasion because, as he said, it was his responsibility to her to show his passion, but he understood and respected her decision. Their time was running out from day one, when he had put his towel down on the grass beside her at the crowded outdoor pool. His fiancée Angela was due to come in the new year. He would be faithful then. He wouldn't need Margrit because he would be busy loving her. Margrit was only his Swiss fling and every day she reminded herself not to fall too hard for him. What she was doing was wrong and missing him afterwards would be her punishment.

A different kind of punishment came her way, because just when Luigi got the news that Angela had booked her train journey, Mr Fasel had her in his sights. She had thought she could handle her boss's attention. Yes, it was uncomfortable sometimes how he behaved, but also a little flattering. And not the sort of thing you could make a fuss about, especially when he only did it when no one was looking. Besides, he praised her work all the time. His affection seemed fatherly. But that was just the lead-up.

It wasn't the only time in her life a man had tried to force himself on her. But it was the most dangerous, because no one else was around. Now, what he did would be called sexual assault or even attempted rape. They were alone in his office. He had asked her to stay late to tidy up after the drinks. She had been bored by the men's conversation and her thoughts had drifted. That was her fault. She should have stayed alert around him, considering the signs. She should never have agreed to be alone with him.

She thought about that for ages afterwards. Was that a code she had missed? Was her willingness to stay a sign of her agreement to something? Should she have refused, made up an appointment or something? But as the only woman in the office, it seemed obvious she should wash and dry the glasses in the little kitchen. The men could hardly be expected to do that when there was a girl on hand. The others had no problem grabbing their coats and rushing off, leaving her with a person they had no reason to fear. But she did.

Her memories of Luigi were polluted by the experience with Herr Fasel. But she wasn't proud of either encounter. How hard it was to steer your destiny with men. There was a limited time, a limited number who pursued you, the bad mixed with the good. So much at stake. Women married much later now, and maybe it was better for them. She hoped so.

11

Ruedi

The place was much busier on a Saturday, even some children running around. Ruedi hoped Mrs Brändli wouldn't be too tired after Peter's visit, though he'd only stayed twenty minutes. He would just hand over the notebook and keep things brief.

The door was held open by a wedge, and he stuck his head in to see her sitting outside on the small patio with a book on her lap, her head hanging down. Her rounded shape, the thinning hair – he could not see any resemblance to the young woman he remembered, who had seemed like a film star to him at the time. It was unlikely she would recall knowing him. Probably best if he didn't bring it up.

Ruedi didn't want to wake her. He stood halfway across the room and took a moment to examine the painting. Yes, now that he looked at it more closely, that was a familiar view – the view from the old house.

'Admiring my son's artwork?'

She startled him. 'Mrs Brändli, I hope I'm not disturbing you. Yes, it's a fine painting. It has something. I've just been speaking to Peter, and earlier to Matthias. We arranged to meet here today.'

'Matthias? Peter said he couldn't come.'

'He couldn't come in. You were asleep and he didn't want to disturb you.'

'Oh, I didn't realise.' There was a note of uncertainty in her voice.

'Yes, so I've spoken to them, but this is not an official visit. Saturdays are for families. I just wanted to drop something off for you.' He stepped through the patio door and held out the notebook.

'Can you help me inside? My legs are very stiff today.'

Ruedi sprang into action, well-practised in transfers like this. He settled her in the orthopaedic chair.

'Sometimes I wheel this thing out there, and sometimes I need a break from it. Prefer to sit in a normal chair. Chair to chair, chair to bed, it's been that kind of day.'

'Well, I won't keep you. I wanted to give you this notebook – it has some writing prompts on this sheet of paper at the front, if you're interested. It's a present. Something you can use if you feel like writing. They say it can be helpful.'

'Oh, that's thoughtful, thank you. I'm not much of a writer.' She put the book on the bed and sighed.

'You gave me a present once. A football.' Ruedi did not know what had come over him. It was as if the young Ruedi had entered the room, demanding to be remembered.

'Pardon?' She looked up at him, her head to one side.

'Do you remember a little boy who stayed with your parents in the late fifties?'

'That's a long time ago. My parents? What makes you speak about my parents?'

'Please, I don't want to upset you. I just wondered if you remembered the boy who stayed in the house in Mendenswil, who was placed with your family. You were working in Bern at the time.'

'There were boys at different times. I don't remember one in particular.'

What a mistake to bring this up. He was confusing her. Ruedi took a step back. 'Then don't worry. Don't give it any more thought. It's just that when I was speaking with Matthias earlier, he mentioned the old family farm.'

'Sit down, man. You look uncomfortable there. Matthias has had a fixation about that place since he was very young. We used to say he should have been born on a farm, that he was made to run free. Not that it's all fun and games living on the land – oh no. We children had to do our bit. Time to play was very much down the list. Children's games were for the schoolyard. At home, we were meant to be useful. Where did you say you grew up?'

Maybe he could steer this into a general chat about the old days. Yes, he could manage that and then extricate himself. 'We moved around a bit but the place I go back to is Wilderswil. I lived there with my mother for three years before we moved back to Bern.'

She had wanted him to have a better choice of apprenticeships, was what she said at the time. But Ruedi knew she found the village claustrophobic. Their neighbours had pieced together their story bit by bit. How could they not gossip when a single mother arrived with her half-grown boy? She felt out of place there. Ruedi had enjoyed those years more than her, stayed close to a family there and kept up the tradition of taking a week off in the summer to help out with the haymaking. The people in the village still knew him and treated him like a local. She enjoyed the more devil-may-care surroundings of the Matte neighbourhood in Bern where all sorts of flotsam washed up from the Aare.

'We did have games, come to think of it,' Margrit went on. 'We played Jass and Gämsch and other card games. And we had a cupboard in the hall with some old board games for winter. No books, though, apart from my mother's detective novels. You were asking about a boy. One Christmas there was a boy, terribly shy, sweet little thing, straight from the home. I taught him some of those games. He had some sort of benefactor.'

'His name was Ruedi.'

'Yes, that's right, Ruedi. He had sandy-coloured hair, the longest eyelashes, small for his age. So cute, he could have been on a chocolate box.'

'You were kind to him. I remember.'

'Such a polite boy. My mother was used to the wilder type.' She seemed to notice him again. 'You knew this child?'

He had to do it now. 'I'm not sure how to tell you this. I was in a children's home from the age of three when I was taken from my mother. The first placement I got when I was ten was with your parents in Mendenswil. I had no idea when I took this case. Your married name... and so much time has passed. But when Matthias mentioned Mendenswil, I remembered you. I remember playing games with you in the front room. You were kind to me.'

'It can't be.'

'It's so long ago, it hardly seems possible that we are the same people who met back then. I was still a child. You were a young woman.'

'It's too long ago. I can't believe... I believe you, but I can't believe the coincidence, the passage of time. It's just too strange.'

'I'm so sorry. We don't have to talk about it if you're not up to it. Can I get you something, call a nurse? Are you all right?'

'I'm fine. You are Ruedi. It's extraordinary. You grew up!'

'I grew old.'

'It happens to the best of us.' She smiled for the first time since he had met her. 'I don't know why I was so slow to remember. You are the one who was reunited with his mother. What a lovely story. And there was that older woman who organised the whole thing. She was high up in politics or something. No, it can't have been politics back then. But she was well connected. She made a big impression on my mother, I can tell you. She wore trousers, I think that was part of it.' She laughed, another first. 'But I can't remember any names. It's maddening. Will you tell me more about your story?'

'If you like. I'd be glad to. But you must be tired.'

'Nonsense. Today they have homemade apricot tart in the canteen. We could have coffee and cake. Would you have time?'

'Yes, I have time. Shall we go down there?'

'I don't usually go down if I can help it. You get waylaid and caught in boring conversations. Besides, my legs.'

'Let me go and fetch us two slices of cake.'

'You're just as obliging as ever, Ruedi. Shall we call each other by our first names?'

Ruedi hesitated. She was older, she was a client, and – he couldn't stop himself from thinking – she was a lady.

'I'm just a farm girl from Mendenswil,' she said, as if she'd read his thoughts. 'You can think about it while you're getting the cake.'

Another memory surfaced. The day of the football. They were in the house at the top of the village, the one Mrs Vogelsang had organised for them. He was not completely comfortable with his mother yet. It must have been shortly after they were reunited. And his mother was not herself. She had been jumpy for days anticipating this important visit. Mrs Vogelsang was coming, and the old woman from the farm where he had lived; at least she seemed like an old woman to him. His mother had him running around the place getting everything ready. He helped her carry the table and chairs outside. There was a tablecloth – borrowed, he supposed. There was cake and fruit he had picked himself. He was dreading spending the day with old biddies, but he didn't dare say that to his mother.

And then she arrived with them, Margrit, making everything special. She had brought a new football from a shop, wrapped in brown paper. He never thought he'd be a boy who could arrive in school with his own football, but she transformed his fortunes. He knew he wouldn't be allowed to play with the ball until the guests were gone, and all the crockery had been cleared away. The whole day – they couldn't have been there the whole day, but it had felt like an eternity – he longed to play with the ball. His mother had tucked it under the sink to remove the temptation.

He took Margrit around the house and perimeter. They put a bottle of wine in the stream to keep it cool. He was proud to show her all the nice places around the little chalet, the stile the neighbour had repaired, their vegetable garden, the rock with the best view through a gap in the trees. And she'd stood on the rock beside him, and what had she said to him? Something about being a great boy, that she'd always thought he was a great boy.

On his way back from the canteen with the tray, he felt a ripple of anxiety cross his chest about what he was starting. If they were going to take a trip down memory lane together, where would it lead? Maybe he should play everything down, not fill her mind with more memories.

Margrit was delighted to see him back. She had cleared her side table and pulled his chair over to it. It was hard to see how she'd managed that, but she was clearly determined to take on her role as hostess. She encouraged him to unload the tray instead of eating off it, and he followed her instructions.

'Can I just say something, Margrit?'

She gave a little clap on hearing him use her first name and nodded her assent.

'As long as you don't neglect your tart.'

'It's very good,' he said, quickly swallowing the first mouthful. 'All I want to say is that I am here to play a very neutral role, to support you and go through the arrangements. And you should be able to treat me like, I don't know, someone delivering a service. You might want to complain, or tell me to leave, or whatever it is. Sometimes we are not as free with people we know. Are you sure you want to talk about the past with me?'

'You're a frank person, Ruedi, and I appreciate that. I'm not worried about you not doing your job well. I haven't forgotten why you're here. For me it's a bonus to remember a part of my life with someone who was there. We'll get back to the other business. Keep eating.'

She observed him for a minute as he ate and drank, taking sips from her coffee cup. 'I'm trying to work out how old you are.'

'Seventy-four,' he said.

'Stop. Do you know that my mother spoke about you when she was dying?'

'Your mother?'

'Yes. We all thought she wanted to die at home, but it turned out that she liked being in hospital. She considered it a luxury. I honestly think she treated it as an outing when she was transferred to the cantonal hospital. She really perked up there for a day or two. But then it became clear after a scan that an operation was out of the question. After that she declined rapidly, too quickly for us to get her a hospice bed. They put her in a private room and let us sit with her. And she spoke about you. There were letters she felt bad about, letters your mother had written. Do you know what that would be about?'

'I never heard about any letters. My mother had no ill will towards your mother. Neither did I. She shouldn't have felt guilty for taking me in.'

'But she wasn't very motherly towards you, was she? I remember complaining to her about that. Could she not be a bit softer with you, I would say. But she wasn't really the soft type in those years. You felt that she was proud of you but also critical. She only turned soft when we left home.'

'Look, I wasn't there long. One full year plus a second winter, I think. Nothing bad happened. I was grieving for a friend of mine from the home who had died just before I was sent away. Not that many children died of childhood illnesses then, even the likes of us. This was the 1950s. I still wonder what happened to him.'

'I'm sorry for your loss, Ruedi.'

Ruedi nodded, not trusting himself to speak. Almost sixty-five years had gone by, and that was the first time anyone had said that to him about Dänu.

12

Margrit

I am old, but am I wise? That was the thought that started the day for Margrit. Instead of reaching for her crossword puzzle book, she took out the new notebook, tucked the loose piece of paper into the back without reading it, and flicked through the empty pages.

Margrit had almost stopped writing on paper since she had got her first mobile phone years earlier. Texts were the ideal means of communication, she had discovered back then. If she thought about it, Margrit hadn't written anything but shopping lists and notes since she gave up her job when pregnant with Peter. Notes to Frederic, notes to the cleaning woman, notes to herself – book hairdressers, order meat for *fondue chinoise* – notes on greeting cards, a note once on a car she had scraped while parking, and notes to teachers excusing the boys from gym class. She had, of course, filled in umpteen forms in recent years, such as the one that got her into this place, various clearance forms for medical interventions and, most relevantly, the form to apply for assisted dying.

But actual writing of actual thoughts – that had become foreign to her. She turned over the notebook, felt the heft of it in her hands. There was nothing of note about this notebook. It was meek, devoid of character or style, made in China. What could you object to? She wrote her name on the inside of the cover.

When you look back on a long life, some things stand out like little peaks on a graph, but it's not the things you might expect.

It may not be your wedding day, the birth of a child, a grad- uation, or some great achievement that comes back to niggle at you or warm your heart. It may not even be traumas lived in your darkest hours, because some things your mind and body prefer to forget. It can be a fleeting memory, something trivial, a remark or a gesture somebody made. Or moments where people revealed their true nature. So, let me see.

She wriggled on the bed to get more comfortable.

I remember once when I was in my forties, being locked in the back of a friend's car because of the child lock. I was with a group of people in two cars coming back from volunteering at the lighting of the Christmas tree in the village we lived in. We were all going for a drink at someone's house. Frederic had ended up in the other car. After the others got out, I lingered in the back seat for just a short time, working up the will to go into a brightly lit house and be a brightly lit person. It was one of those moments I used to have where I fantasised about walking away. About getting out of the car and walking back down the hill to the village and catching the evening bus away from there, never to return. I don't know if I replayed the whole fantasy on that occasion, but it usually ended with me somewhere warm, on a ferry about to leave port to an island destination. Obviously that wasn't a warm time of year, and the sea was seven hundred kilometres away, but that was the fantasy, which had become detailed over time. Suddenly, the light changed as the front door closed. They were all gone. Eight people, including my husband and neighbours we had known for years, and with them the Lehmanns, who also had a son in Zurich with Matthias, shooting up heroin in Platzspitz, for all we knew, at that very moment.

I could have leaned forward and beeped the horn to get their attention, but I remained passive. I don't know if that's a decision; they say it is. I think of it as a reaction, not entirely voluntary. I thought the mistake would immediately come to light, someone would dash out within a moment, and I would be brought inside triumphantly as the rescued damsel. That we would all find it funny and laugh in the forced way that people laugh when they don't know how to amuse each other anymore.

So how is that for a memory to come and bother me forty years later? They did not miss me for a full ten minutes, and it was not even Frederic who raised the alarm. One of the children of the house, arriving home, squeezing her bike between the two cars in the driveway, got quite a fright when she saw my anxious moon face looking out at her from the car. A meaningless little humiliation.

She should have been able to think of a more pleasant memory. But where were the peaks? All she could summon was a chain of small repeated tasks, wiping a particular table over and over, opening the letter box, taking a teabag from the same tin, popping out those osteoporosis tablets she'd taken for the last thirty-five years; the background noise of memory. What other notes rang out? She saw herself sitting on the stairs by the front door, getting cold, waiting for her child who hadn't come home. That time she'd really thought he would turn up dead. The cat came and sat on her lap to keep her warm. She cried a tear of gratitude.

Come now, Margrit, there must be happy scenes. What about the time before the house was built when they lived in that little apartment near the station? Yes, she'd go there.

I'm watching from my kitchen window as an elderly nun in the convent garden across the road, wearing a long apron, tends the vegetables. I feel glad for her and glad for myself, sipping my tea while the people walk downhill to the train station on the sunny side of the street, unaware of the pretty garden right there behind the wall. It is a quiet moment when the baby is having his nap. Soon he will wake, and it will be playtime or pureed carrot time or milk time or pram time. I have the whole day worked out.

In that place, when I stood in the kitchen looking out, my parents were still alive – far away but alive. I even had a grandmother. My baby was home safe with me, and there was another one on the way. They were both as good as gold, though not many people knew about the second one swimming and dreaming his way towards us. Everyone remarked on how easy baby Peter was. Because we are happy, I would think but not say.

She couldn't really say she was wise. Just that she saw her mistakes more clearly now. There was a line from the Act of Contrition about sinning: *in what I have done and what I have failed to do.* Failing to do: that's where she went wrong. She turned the page.

I had my own car for forty-five years. I was a bit late getting lessons, but I was glad when I finally could drive. I felt like a new person, driving around dropping things off, visiting people, buying things. The long stage when it was all about the children. Trips to the doctor and dentist, birthday parties, buying clothes and shoes, driving them to the train, picking them up from the train. They had football matches in every far-flung corner of the canton. Hundreds of football matches between them over many years. Countless times, I took the right off the main road leading to our suburban village; there was an old bus shelter there, but the bus came along rarely. One day, coming home towards dusk, I saw a woman standing there. She had a lot of bags with her, strewn around on the wet ground. I couldn't tell if it was shopping or just plastic bags of possessions. She was about my age but an outsider in some instantly recognisable way. The rain wasn't very heavy, but she had no umbrella, and her hair and the shoulders of her coat were wet. She wasn't standing under the shelter but closer to the road, stretching out her hand for a lift. I didn't have much time after taking the turn to see her, assess the situation and make a decision, but the truth is, I did have enough time. And I wanted to be the one to stop and give her a lift. I wanted to do that, but some little fear held me back. All the way home, I hated myself for being inhibited, for having become a person who felt unable to live my life freely.

Where is the good in it all? In the rituals more than the deeds, perhaps. Frederic said every man should build a house, plant a tree, and have a son. There is no rule for women. I planted a blackcurrant bush, the start of a thirty-year pact, a privilege. Pulling the branches, feeling my primate fingers efficiently doing the work they evolved to do, just the right pressure to separate little clusters of the plump berries from the stalk. The ping of the berries hitting the plastic bowl at the start, the plop as they land on many layers of their brethren. Picking out the stray ants and the brown geometric beetles. Avoiding the earwigs. The anticipation of the jam, the bush gradually being stripped of its juicy offering in the dappled shade, the air warm around me, and soft grass a cushion for my feet. One blackcurrant bush picked twenty, thirty times. Continuity as the children grow and one day leave. The feeling of connection to the world. The reminder that nature knows what it's doing and that it has allowed a place for you. The bush failed one year; that, too, is part of the story. But I still have the essence of that untroubled day of blackcurrant picking with me, regardless of what year it was.

13

Ruedi

The third visit anywhere is when familiarity sets in. Ruedi picked up two takeaway coffees in the café, and nodded in greeting to the floating residents and staff he passed on his way to Margrit's room. He had brought the *Bund* with him to show her an article about Bernese nightlife in the 1960s. Again, the door was propped open, and this time she beckoned him over by holding up a slice of tart on a plate.

'It's cherry today.'

'Nice.' He put the coffees on the table and emptied out the creamers and sugar sachets from his pockets. As they mixed and poured, Margrit told him about her meeting with the home director that morning.

'He wanted to know my reasons.'

'Aha.'

'The most vast and intimate of subjects. Most people cannot explain why they carry on living without resorting to clichés. Why should I explain why I choose not to carry on?'

'Is that what you told him?'

'No, I gave him some clichés. Never leave home without them. Tired of life, that's what you people from Depart say. That's a legitimate reason. And I mentioned this valley of tears, in case he was a religious type.'

'And was he satisfied?'

'Enough to leave me alone. These cherries are great. Next week they'll have plums.'

'We're working our way through all the summer fruit.' Ruedi wiped his mouth on a paper napkin and caught himself thinking: *her last summer.*

'Tell me, Ruedi, have you been with someone on their deathbed? I mean apart from this line of work.'

'Oh yes – my wife, my mother. There was a man who had a heart attack on the train once.'

'I'm sorry to make you recall these things.'

'No, please, carry on.' He opened his hands, palms upwards.

'What's strange is that you know the person is close to death, but how close? Will it be hours or another day or more? It's the ultimate suspense. Did you ever read *Buddenbrooks?* There is a death scene in that, appalling. It would chill you to the bone. We did the book in school. I looked it up recently, I have the time. Old Mrs Buddenbrook's agony goes on for days.'

'But that kind of thing doesn't happen anymore. Don't be afraid, Margrit.'

'I'm not afraid of a bad death – I'm just giving an extreme example. I simply want out when it suits me and not years after I'm ready. Eighty-six years: that's enough life for me.'

Ruedi rested his hand on his cheek as he considered this last statement. His vision blurred, seeing only the merged colours of the curtain. He could picture the scene of Maria's last hours so clearly. Machines gone, her hands still on the turned-down sheet, the noble profile he knew by heart, and the last time she looked at him with unseeing eyes.

He had missed his mother's death by minutes, when he slipped out of the room to look for a coffee. Wandering the corridors in vain, he ended up drinking from a bathroom tap. Oh, the recriminations he subjected himself to when he came back to find her lifeless body. But even the dying themselves cannot know their last breath. They are being pulled away by a gentle tide, and finally they let go.

Both experiences were peaceful. Watching them breathing, in and out, deep and slow, the pauses, not believing it would or could finally stop. How was it possible? The most natural thing in the world. Not a thing – a process, he remembered the doctors saying. He became aware of Margrit's presence again, her body angled forward in expectation.

'Let's go out on the patio,' she said.

He jumped to attention and got her settled.

'Now, you give me some clichés in favour of living,' she said, turning to look at the garden, as plain as could be on this side of the building, with a tall laurel hedge blocking any view.

'There's all of this – life, growth, renewal, beauty.' He gestured towards the grass.

'Beauty?' She raised an eyebrow and he smiled.

'Well, you know, nature.'

'I'm sorry, Ruedi. It is a good one. Though when I think of how humans brutalise nature while claiming to love it… Never mind. The warmth of the sun, excluding the odd heatwave, is a joy. Flowers, fields, mountains, valleys. I'm a summer person – I love colour, blue skies, swims in the lake, summer food and clothes. But can you imagine the relief of not having to face another winter? To be gone before the leaves fall. That's part of my wish. To escape the winter once and for all. I'm tired of winter. Tired of facing it, submitting to it, enduring those cold, empty days year after year. I don't believe anybody likes winter.'

'But it never lasts, isn't that the point? Spring comes around again – the snowdrops, crocuses, daffodils – life returns.'

'True, that usually keeps us going.' She didn't look convinced.

'I need to ask a question. Official business. It's about your sons.'

'Ah.'

'Do you want them there at the end? I mean in the room?'

'I have thought about that, and the answer is I'd rather not. They would make it about them. This may sound harsh, but I have paid my dues as a mother. I'm fond of Matthias and Peter, but I can see that the visits here have become a duty to them. Look at the fiasco last week. Now Peter wants to reschedule. I can release us all from these ties of duty. Isn't the death of your parents a liberation of sorts? Finally, the original debt, the greatest one of all, is cancelled.'

'And what do they say?'

'Matthias has phoned but he will not engage on the subject. He blocks it out. Perhaps he is ashamed of me. Sometimes he gets emotional, in the moment. But his tears are dry before he hangs up, I know it. He doesn't like to be left, makes a drama of it. Do you know that when we are together, he reproaches me for wrongs I did to him in the past? When I think of all we did for him! Talk about second chances – he got a hundred chances.'

'I'm sorry, Margrit. He probably came of age at a bad time. I'll never forget those crazy years. We saw a lot of addicts on the trains. It was an epidemic – and some people just caught it. In my experience, they weren't necessarily the bad ones, more the weak ones.'

'I know all those arguments. I don't really blame him. Nevertheless, I am more than ready to lay down that particular burden. He started at seventeen or eighteen. What is that, forty years ago? A lifetime. He didn't finish his military service or his apprenticeship, nothing. He's been a "case" since then. Though I will say this: he was a delightful child. Loving, caring. He cared about every little ladybird. The teachers loved him. We thought he was special – that pretty little face.'

Ruedi reached down to pull at some spindly little weeds in the flowerpot at his side, while Margrit dabbed her eyes with a tissue.

'Tell me about your wife, Ruedi.'

'Maria?'

'Yes. I'm talking too much.'

'I'm not sure. How can you sum a person up anyway?'

'Try. Just tell me about her character. Was she a warm person?'

'Yes, warm is a good word to describe her. The Italian way. She was also full of certainty. That's what made me interested in her when we first met. As a young man, I was unsure of myself. I never had that certainty most men seemed to have. I never expressed an opinion. I just watched and listened. It felt like I had so much to learn – about how to be in the world. My history, you know. But Maria was different. She was two years older than me, worked as a hairdresser. She knew what was fair and unfair, and she would say so. She talked back to people, senior people. She had a plan for us. I suppose you could say she was more of a leader. And the plan worked for a while, it did. Until she got MS. That was something Maria could not overcome with her certainty.'

Margrit gave a sympathetic murmur. 'And how did the illness start?'

'It was when Alessandra was still a toddler. Maria first started to notice this awful tiredness. At Alessandra's bedtime, she would lie on the floor beside the little bed – Alessandra was always a terrible sleeper, resisted falling asleep. It would be early evening, seven or half past, and it started to happen more often than not that Maria would not appear again after putting Alessandra to bed. When I went to check, I would find her asleep on the floor, and she was so tired, she would need to be helped to bed. We put it down to motherhood, winter, low iron, that kind of thing. She reduced her hours. But always this exhaustion.

'And one day, we were out for a walk together – a day out in Elfenau, you know the place. And we stopped at a bench for our sandwiches and flask of coffee, and Alessandra was collecting chestnuts, I remember that, the most gorgeous rich shiny chestnuts. It was a happy moment. But when we went to leave, Maria couldn't get up. It was as if she was drunk – her legs were no use. With the help of a student and his girlfriend, we got her to the café, and the manager there took a break to drive us home. So kind. That's when we first went to the doctor.'

'I'm so sorry, Ruedi.'

'It was just one of those things. From that point on, other symptoms became more noticeable, like blurred vision and balance problems, but it took another year to get a diagnosis. MS became part of our marriage. Attacking her while I looked on helplessly. The medicines are so much better now. If only. Anyway, it changed us both. It changed Alessandra too.'

'I can't imagine.'

'I'm making it sound terrible. But we got on with things. We enjoyed life on a smaller scale – what counted as a good day changed. You know the expression "you cut your cloth"? That's what we did. Maria still worked for quite a while. Her boss was understanding. When her hands became too clumsy to cut and style hair, she was put on the desk, welcoming customers, taking calls, sorting supplies, that kind of thing. She cooked with Alessandra's help, sitting on a stool and giving Alessandra the finer jobs. You'd be amazed how much a small child can learn. More physical things like changing sheets and washing floors, I did those. Maria spent a lot of time in bed, resting, listening to the radio. Neighbours helped, too, taking Alessandra to play. One woman from Valais was very kind – every Wednesday she'd offer to bring Maria back something from the market. The progression was slow. One stick, two sticks, crutches. By the time Alessandra finished her apprenticeship, Maria was in a wheelchair. She was proud to have held out that long.'

'And you were proud of her?'

'Yes, proud of her courage, even though it could make things harder sometimes.'

'Thank you for telling me about Maria. I would like to have known her.'

'She would have liked you.'

This time, Margrit looked away as Ruedi dabbed his eyes.

14

Margrit

When Margrit read over what she'd written the last time, she felt a little queasy. *Nothing we write means anything*, she thought. *It is just a snapshot.*

She unfolded the page of instructions. There was some guff about a life audit, a record of the highs and lows of each decade of your life. *Can be helpful… process of acceptance…* Maybe her sister-in-law Usha would have believed in this. But what else had she to do today? Decade by decade – *let's see.*

1–10

Three younger brothers born in the family. Dirty nappies steeping in the bucket, lots of crying, helping feed whoever was in the high chair. War in the distance; Papi away, Mami tired.

A boy in my class died in a fall. I remember his body laid out on his parents' bed wearing his altar boy smock, and me sitting on one of the chairs against the wall, trying to pray like the others. A younger sibling, not much more than a toddler, was horsing around. He knocked the bedroom door open several times looking for attention. Each time, the door hitting the bed made the little corpse jolt, until an adult snatched the bothersome child away. He really is dead, then, is what I remember thinking, my mind like an exploding star following all the implications.

A never-seen great aunt in a convent sent me a beautiful silver cross for my Communion. One of the boys buried it in the garden as part of a treasure game and couldn't remember where.

Polishing the boys' shoes for Mass and realising they would never have to do the same for me. Clearing their plates, sweeping the floor of their room, fuming.

Pigs, always pigs. The noise, the smell, the insistence of them. Trying not to care about the piglets. The kindly old sow I called Rosalee. I fancied that she understood me.

This is not an audit, Margrit thought. These are the ramblings of a half-senile, half-literate fool. She threw the pen down and closed the book. Even writing slowly with lots of breaks, Margrit had a terrible cramp in her hand. A good thing it was lunchtime.

The after-lunch nap was one of the simple pleasures of old age. She couldn't deny it. But she wouldn't admit it either. No need – no one would ever ask.

When she woke up, Margrit made herself comfortable on the bed, pulled over the trolley table and tackled 11–20. Brevity this time.

Best friend Thérèse whose mother went crazy. Her lovely black hair. Standing by Thérèse while the other girls ostracised her. Being inexplicably dropped by Thérèse when the new term started.

All the talk of the scholarship. That summer minding the weird cousins and coming home with lice, blaming Mami.

Getting into secretarial college. The row between Mami and Papi about my future.

The end-of-summer party at the lake. First kiss.

The job in Loeb. Buying the yellow handbag with my employees' discount. Best money ever spent.

Horrible landlady, forget her name. Nice room. Sunday visits home.

Waiting for something interesting to happen.

Did anything interesting happen? Not really. There was no way of disguising it, Margrit had led an uneventful life. She paused, and as soon as her concentration lapsed, the grating sounds of the home surged up again around her. Various trolleys rumbling, doors closing, hurrying footsteps, voices calling. It was all so dull, dull beyond belief. *I've been patient all my life*, she thought. *Can't I be afforded a little impatience at last?*

Her twenties were a little muddled. Different men, different jobs, that constant feeling of insecurity. Until Frederic. And that was a big part of the attraction. She was like one of those champion women swimmers who made it onto the news in the old days, the ones who swam the English Channel. The constant effort of it, too far to go back but no shore in sight. And then Frederic came along beside her in a boat, and all she had to do was get in. No more struggling to make ends meet, to navigate past the sharks. An apartment first, then a house, that was what was in store for her if she just stopped trying. No wonder they all gave up. Not like the women nowadays who actually had interesting jobs and earned real money. They had no idea. Tentatively she turned the page.

21–30

With L. at the Marzili Pool. His smile, his hands.

The business with Mr F. Mami confronting him and saving the day.

Changing jobs three times, ending up at the Historical Museum. Meeting Frederic at the Ka-We-De skating rink, Hollywood style.

Wedding. My father's pride, the slight feeling of disappointment.

First miscarriage, second miscarriage. The holiday in Como. Pregnancy and birth of Peter.

Third miscarriage. Pregnancy and birth of Matthias. Building the house. Leaving the apartment.

Mami's breast cancer.

L. coming to fix the sink.

It felt disloyal to even think about Luigi. But instead of picturing Frederic at the skating rink coming towards her outside the buvette with a *café fertig* in each hand, instead of remembering that sweet taste of sugar, schnapps and coffee on his lips when they had their first kiss on the way home, she found it was Luigi who appeared in her memory. They had parted before she met Frederic, each taking with them a debt of unspent passion. Margrit had wanted to be open, modern and carefree, but she missed him desperately. She thought she'd never see him again. Until, one day, she did.

Oh God, why think about this now? Luigi turning up at her house in the middle of the day to replace a cracked sink. She was still tidying up the kitchen after lunch. She didn't even bother to take off her apron when the bell rang. He arrived with an apprentice, made no sign of recognising her in front of the boy, it was all *Sie* this and *Sie* that, and his eyes on her the whole time, spitting sparks. The little one was asleep in his cot upstairs, and Peter was messing about outside in the sandpit. When Luigi sent the lad away to walk down to the village for an ice cream for the child, playing the soft Italian family man, she knew exactly what he was doing. They faced each other in the sitting room, breathless, Peter's voice carrying through the open window, singing while he played with his trucks. She locked the patio door. There would only be minutes. The most passionate minutes of her life, she could now say with certainty, from a distance of almost sixty years. Standing up against the wall by the fireplace, still wearing the apron. The guilt kept Margrit cemented in her marriage for good.

15

Ruedi

Ruedi had the laundry room from six in the morning to six in the evening on Wednesdays. He didn't mind leaving the evenings and weekends to his working neighbours.

Morning light streamed into the sitting room and he opened the balcony door and his bedroom window to allow the coolest air of the day to circulate. As he stripped his bed and moved around the apartment gathering up towels and tea towels, he thought of the conversation with Margrit. Tired of life. Would he ever feel the same?

Already now, in his early seventies, when on some days his only arrangement was with the washing machine in the basement, he felt his own weariness. He stuffed the bundle of laundry into an IKEA bag, threw in the box of powder and headed downstairs.

On the way past the letter boxes, he checked for post. The newspaper was there, a couple of bills and a begging letter from a charity he had once supported. Nothing to get excited about. He pulled open the basement door and was hit by a strong smell of detergent, a blend of different brands. Why did people have to use so much of the stuff? Once the wash was on, he went to fetch the basket from his storage compartment. There was no room for it in the apartment so it lived down here with his tools, beer-brewing buckets, old flower pots, suitcases and other travel bags, Maria's jam-making glassware, the dog's bed, a box of winter shoes and an assortment of outdoor equipment including a pair of collapsible picnic chairs he had never opened. He tucked one of the chairs under his arm and took a minute to inspect his bicycle. A layer of dust covered the saddle and the tyres were a little soft. He hated to neglect it, but it would make him sadder to spruce it up for nothing.

A year before, on his way to a physio appointment for a stiff neck, his front wheel had caught in a tram line and he had toppled over, landing hard on his left shoulder. A lot more physio was needed after that, but the worst thing was that Ruedi lost his cycling nerve. He hadn't got on the bike since, and Alessandra did everything she could to discourage him from trying. One day she got him to take the bicycle outside to be photographed. But he hadn't given her the all-clear to sell it online yet.

The shortest wash cycle was one hour and eighteen minutes, which gave Ruedi good time to read the paper over breakfast. The sunlight in his apartment was so lovely, he delayed putting down the blinds until the second wash was finished at nine. He left the sheets in the tumbler and brought the towels up to dry on a clothes horse on the balcony. The day had become unnaturally still, the freshness of the morning quickly smothered by the advance of the hot sun.

One court case story in the paper unsettled him. It was about a man who befriended a girl online in secret. He persuaded her to meet him without telling anyone and camped with her in a deserted area for several nights. His defence was that she was a willing participant. She said she was frightened the whole time she was with him and could only leave when hikers came along and stopped for a chat. It seemed that every day brought a new story about harm being done to women and children. He wished he was some kind of superhero who could find these men and hurt them back. If anyone ever touched Florian, he would not let it pass. These thoughts drained him. He went to check on his third and last wash.

In the hall on the way down, he met Mrs Oliveira from upstairs and they agreed that it was too hot. Not wanting the conversation to end, he sympathised about forest fires in Portugal, another item he had noticed in the paper, and she told him one had come very close to her hometown the previous summer.

'There are so many problems in the world. I don't know what to worry about most,' she said, picking up her shopping bags again. She looked cheerful despite her words. 'Anyway,' she added, 'you've still got to shop and you've got to cook.'

'And wash your clothes,' Ruedi replied, and they shared a smile.

It was the longest he'd ever spoken to his neighbour. They wished each other a good day and Ruedi felt that they both really meant it. He could still have a good day too. Change the direction. He tapped to check for the storage key in his pocket. At least he could rub the dust off his bicycle and pump up the tyres. There must be a quiet, flat place he could take it for a trial run, the school yard for instance. He could be back before the real heat of the day kicked in.

16

Margrit

Margrit had booked the home's private sitting room, mainly used by grieving families or for small birthday gatherings. She had only used it once before, when two old neighbours, miraculously still alive, had visited together. It had been an obvious duty call, and she hadn't wanted them poking around in her bedroom. God, that had been a long ninety minutes.

'You're getting popular.' Nadja was standing at the open door, waiting to be invited in.

'Hello, Nadja. Thanks for making the time.'

'At your service. What's the plan?' There were two sofas and three armchairs in the room, arranged around the walls. Well out of reach of any of the seats was an oval-shaped coffee table in the middle of the room. It looked like the furniture had been put together with the brief to avoid social interaction. Nadja immediately started tugging at the chair closest to her.

'They call it a sitting room, but it looks too much like a waiting room,' said Margrit. 'There will be four of us. I thought we could use the armchairs and one sofa, make a little circle with the table in the middle. Is it not too heavy for you?'

'No, they're on castors; it's fine.' Margrit saw that Nadja was a person who could never admit to anything being too difficult. As Nadja puffed and heaved, Margrit admired the woman's gumption. For a brief moment, she allowed herself to imagine having a capable daughter like this. Someone who could have civilised the boys a bit. Someone Matthias could have confided in. Pointless nonsense!

Nadja straightened a few angles, moved a vase from a cabinet onto the coffee table. 'There,' she said. 'It's all yours.'

Other old women used terms of endearment for younger people and Margrit would like to have had that knack of motherly geniality. Thank you, pet. Thank you, love. But it was no use starting now. She said her thank yous, and Nadja bustled off with a carefree wave.

The three men were due to arrive any minute. It struck Margrit that she didn't really have any female allies in her life, despite living in a building which was at least eighty per cent female. Usha was the last woman she had felt very close to. Poor Usha. Most friendships in her life had had their season and then faded away. When that happened, they might keep seeing each other out of habit or politeness, but the friendship was not really alive anymore, and it was only a matter of time before the gaps would be stretched so far apart that the former friends could neatly abandon each other. With Usha, it had been quite different – joyous.

She noticed Ruedi hovering at the door, a habit he had never lost. She feared Peter and Matthias would crowd him out completely with the masculine confidence they had inherited from their father. Despite years of ruin, Matthias still expected people to shut up and listen to him.

'You found the room. Come in!'

'How are you, Mrs Brändli?' That was their compromise, *Du* in private and *Sie* in front of other people, a good enough arrangement.

'Nervous, Mr Lappert,' she said.

'I think we're as ready as we can be. Remember, no excuses. We're not here to debate your wishes.'

'Indeed. Look, I'll put you here, to my right. It's not as low as the other chairs, see.'

'This is perfect. *Courage*.' Ruedi placed his hand over hers and gave her a look filled with kindness. He pulled his hand away as the voices of Margrit's sons in the corridor announced their arrival.

They looked well, considering, Margrit thought, as she watched the hand-shaking and accepted kisses on the cheek. Considering what? The hand of time, for one thing; the vicissitudes of life and all that. She was glad that neither man reminded her very much of Frederic. Matthias looked like Frederic's brother Franz, and Peter looked like her brother Hugo. A funny genetic party trick.

Peter sank down heavily on the sofa while Matthias walked over to the window. He still had the instinct to look for an emergency exit from every situation.

'Did you drive together?' she asked.

'Yes, well, my chauffeur here picked me up at the local station.' Matthias gestured mockingly at his brother. 'Didn't trust me to make my own way here. An e-car no less – we floated up. I know the whole sales pitch now.'

Peter shook his head dismissively. 'I wasn't taking any chances this time.' Then he clasped his hands together, and took a moment to look at each person in turn, making sure he had everyone's attention. 'I just wanted to say that we think this meeting is a good idea. We' – he nodded towards his brother – 'accept my mother's wishes. With some regret.'

'Not equal regret,' Matthias said.

'We're not religious, anyway. I've seen a lot of the older genera-tion go in the last couple of decades. We all have. Parents' friends, parents of friends, neighbours, colleagues. There doesn't seem to be a good option, certainly not any easy option. It's just the timing. It feels somewhat too soon.'

Matthias cut across him again. 'We said we respect her decision, there's no need for speeches. Let's ask this guy what the plan is. That's what I want to know. I mean, where will it happen? When?'

'Would you like to start, Margrit?'

'No, you.'

'We have a date, and a time. 15 September at two in the afternoon.'

The boys were very still but would not meet her eyes. Margrit felt an unexpected twinge of shame rising in her throat, but she swallowed it back down. Ruedi checked on her before continuing.

'The director of the home, Mr Balsiger, has kindly agreed for the procedure to take place here. That is a very recent change of policy, and we have all been asked to be discreet. Mrs Brändli would like you to be here, in this room. She would like you to be nearby but not actually present for the end. Mr Balsiger will be present, the doctor of course, and myself.'

'Not present? You prefer to die with strangers at your bedside?' Matthias stood behind Peter with his hands on the sofa back.

'We find it can be better for the family and the person taking leave. It depends—'

'This is not taking leave – this is death, the end. I know you're a fortress, Mami, but this is taking it too far.'

'It's a very personal decision.'

'Thank you,' Peter said, cutting Ruedi off with an impatient gesture. 'Mother, we will respect your wishes. You have our attention, if that's what you wanted, and you have our compliance. So, good for you.'

'Why don't you say something?' Matthias was trying hard to keep his temper in check.

Margrit sighed. 'I'm sorry. I'm sorry things turned out this way. I'll be gone soon, and it's for the best. Don't feel bad for me, and please don't feel bad for yourselves. As you said, everyone around us is dying. So let's not make a drama of it.'

She turned to Ruedi. 'I have a headache. Please take me back to my room.'

*

'Are they gone?'

'Yes.'

'Are they all right?'

'Ahm. Well. Matthias said he wanted to walk back to the station. And Peter has an issue with the date. He's asked if we can move it forward a week.'

'Is this about his New Zealand trip?'

'Yes.'

'My son has become one of those Swiss people who worships the God of travel. Because his life here is unbearable.' She pressed a fist against her mouth. 'A week earlier. Will it work for the others?'

'It should work. I can find out. But will it work for you?'

'That's three weeks away. I suppose so. Can I ask you a favour?'

'Of course.'

'Could you drive me to Mendenswil one day between now and then?'

'You want to see the old place?'

'Yes. One last time. Maybe I am sentimental after all.'

'I don't have a car, but—'

'Oh no, then don't worry, it's fine.'

'But what I want to say is that I can get a car. My daughter can get me one through her car-sharing network or whatever it is. I want to. I'd like to. We can take a picnic.'

'A picnic! Thank you, Ruedi. You are very kind.'

'It will be interesting for me too. After all this time.'

'I'd like you to understand about my sons. You probably think we are awful people.'

'You don't have to explain anything to me. I know family relationships can be difficult.'

'Difficult? Peter once accused me of being a mechanical mother. A mechanical mother! And I found that, surprisingly for him, such an interesting observation. It was maybe closer to the truth than I wanted to admit. I wasn't my true self with my boys. They might have thrived in a different home, possibly with Frederic's people. They seemed to turn out much more like them.'

'Margrit, you are being too hard on yourself.'

'No wonder Peter's wife Nathalie doesn't like me. Kept the children from me, and I don't even know whether Peter tried to prevent that. I was no mechanical grandmother, that's for sure. Maybe she made him resent that. All around me my contemporaries were fawning over grandchildren and minding them two or three days a week, talking of nothing else. Peter and Nathalie kept moving further away, and I was lucky if I saw those kids two or three times a year. They look like her, by the way.'

'You know something, if you don't mind me changing the subject, you were a real looker in your day. That's how I remember you.'

Margrit realised she was burdening him with her lament, so she let the compliment have the desired effect, knocking Ruedi's arm with the back of her hand. 'What would you remember? You were only a boy!'

'You had something special, Margrit. Don't deny it. And now, I should go and catch Balsiger before he goes off duty. I'll be back very soon.'

Maybe she had been good-looking, but if so, it had been a mixed blessing. The most beautiful person she'd known had been her sister-in-law Usha. She should spend more time thinking about her instead. They used to see each other every week when Marcel moved back to Bern from New York. The highlight of her week. Usha struggled with life in Switzerland, the constraints, the way they treated her, the way she couldn't be herself anymore. She used the word parochial, and Margrit used to think, *Surely I am the most parochial person you know*, but they had found something in common, some kind of shared alienation and unhappiness. Which, wonderfully, they had been able to defuse in each other.

Margrit had never had that closeness with Frederic or even with her favourite brother Marcel. After Usha died, she never found anyone else who had her qualities. She doubted there could be such a person – unless Ruedi. The way she could talk to him... it was similar. A parting gift, perhaps.

17

Ruedi

'You've caught me at a good time,' Carmen said. 'I'm stuck waiting for a chicken breast to marinate. One day, I'll lead a life where I remember early enough to marinate things in advance.'

'I'm on the balcony, having a beer. Haven't even thought about dinner yet. It's too hot to eat.'

'So, how is it going with the lady of the manor? You have a date now, don't you?'

'Actually, there's a lot to tell. Yes, we have a date: 8 September.'

'Three weeks away – that's close.'

'Yes, it is. Dr Boschung is lined up to do it. The director of the home has given his agreement, and the next of kin, the two sons, have been informed. I was there for the family meeting on Thursday.'

'And how is she?'

'She is sure. Ready.'

'And the paperwork is all done?'

'Pretty much. Everything is in order, you could say.'

'And yet? What's the matter, Ruedi? I can hear it in your voice.'

'What can you hear?'

'Doubt.'

'There is something I haven't had a chance to tell you.'

'What?'

Ruedi picked at the label on his beer. 'It's the connection with the client. I mean, I discovered I have a connection with her from the past.' For years, he had hardly ever spoken of his childhood circumstances and suddenly, it seemed that he was telling everyone. He tried to give her the short version.

'The thing is that we met before when I was a child and she was a young woman. Long story but full disclosure, I suppose. Both my mother and I spent our childhood years in care – she was Yenish – but I ended up spending some time living with Mrs Brändli's parents, and I used to see her when she visited home. And there was at least one other time we saw each other. She came to my birthday tea when I was back living with my mother and gave me a football.'

'Oh my goodness.'

'Well, I looked at the code of conduct, and I didn't see anything explicitly about knowing the person. It says it shouldn't be someone in your circle, but you can't really count a brief acquaintance over sixty years ago as someone in your circle.'

'I agree. So why do you feel so concerned?'

'It's just that I agreed – um, we made a plan. It hasn't happened yet, but there is an arrangement.'

'What arrangement?'

'There's a certain rapport. And she has a wish. Basically, her wish is to visit her old home, the place where I stayed in the countryside. And I have agreed to take her there.'

'Aha. So you're going on an excursion together.'

'Yes.'

'Like friends.'

'Somewhat like friends. But she might not be able to go otherwise. She isn't comfortable with that many people. I don't think she has anyone else she can ask.'

'What about the two sons?'

'Not cut out for that. No, they wouldn't understand, and she wouldn't enjoy it.'

'But you're not saying that you're closer to her than her sons.'

'I wouldn't make a claim like that, but the relationship with them is not easy.'

'Well, that is interesting. And could be a transgression in a way. What we absolutely have to guard against is any suggestion of undue influence. Please don't tell me this old connection would be sentimental enough towards you for her to leave you something in her will.'

'I don't think that would occur to her – it hadn't occurred to me.'

'This is really awkward, Ruedi. But with my supervisor hat on, I would recommend that you don't socialise with a client outside of meetings about the core business.'

'The business of her death.'

'Of accompanying her through this process in a practical way. You're a liaison with the organisation. Day trips to the countryside don't fit into that.'

'I've already said I'll do it. Carmen, she's expecting this from me. I think I'm the best person to take her there.'

'To the chateau?'

'It's not a chateau, it's a small former pig farm in the Fribourg Oberland.'

'You know what? I'm not actually going to order you not to go. Because you and I also have a connection, which we probably shouldn't have. What can I advise? Don't put it in your timesheet.'

'Thanks, Carmen.'

'Hey, Ruedi, just one thing. Don't get attached, OK?'

18

Margrit

The cool air of the fan passed back and forth over her body like a blessing. Margrit let the rhythm soothe her. If sleep wouldn't come, there was another kind of oblivion to be found in the monotony. It was the third day of the heatwave. The third day of hunkering indoors behind closed shutters, waiting in vain for the evening air to cool. Margrit felt like a sea animal stranded on dry land. She longed to be immersed in water. She loved water. Why hadn't she sought it out more in her life? She saw herself at five or six years old, with her father, down by the river at the end of the long field. She'd followed him about all morning while Mami was busy with the little ones. It was turning into another hot, dusty day. He wasn't always in the mood for her company, but when he was, he made her feel like a proper assistant. The ground was so dry they had to water the corn. He dragged the hoses from the water cart and laid them out between the rows. Her job was to check for kinks and then to wait at the cart with the horse. She must have slowed him down. She was getting tired and hungry, but she didn't want to stop helping.

There they were, down at the river, almost the whole field done, when they heard the call for lunch. Her father unhitched the horse and led him over to the water's edge for a drink. Then he sat down on a rock and took off his boots. Margrit wasn't allowed in the river ever, even at the edge where the water was only knee-deep.

A child in the village had drowned many years earlier, and with four children under six, her mother was afraid to take them there.

That day, Margrit watched her father as he rolled up his trousers and took off his shirt. It was like the beginning of a grand ceremony. She took off her loose dress, and they waded into the river hand in hand. Papi bent over so she could scoop up water in her hands and pour it over him. The more he yelped, the more she laughed. Mami would be cross, they both knew that, but they both dipped their heads in completely and smiled at each other as the water ran down their faces.

Today was the day of her outing with Ruedi. They wouldn't be able to get down to the river, that was obvious. She hadn't bothered to go there all through the years, and now she couldn't. Whenever she had visited her brother Hugo and his wife, the entire time was spent in the kitchen, and it was an endurance test. No one thought of going to walk around the land. The wife would have seen that as snooping, coveting.

But when her parents were still alive, she did show Frederic the prettiest places, including the river, which had the advantage of being well out of sight of the rest of the farm. There they did what newlyweds do if they get the chance. She remembers the yellow dress she was wearing, how she unexpectedly got her period. They washed each other in the river afterwards, and he gave her his handkerchief for the way back. Frederic had no shame about bodies, and that was a lesson she was glad to learn from him.

Margrit realised she was crying. She hadn't cried for Frederic in such a long time. For anyone. The tears wouldn't stop. Her body felt so heavy on the bed, pinned down. And all at once, a pressure in her head, in her chest, in her throat. Fear prickled across her skin. What was happening? These were new sensations. Her right hand reached automatically for the alarm on her wristband. She was about to press. The pressure on her body released. She relaxed her hand, too. What was she doing calling for help? A woman who already had a date with death in her diary. How ridiculous, Margrit thought. Suddenly, she couldn't stand the movement of the fan anymore. She sat up to turn it off. She just had to lean across the bedside table to get to the switch. But the movement was too sudden. Margrit, the fan, the table, her bottle of water, her glasses, her notebook, and her box of tissues all came crashing down. On the ground, she did not feel dazed but wide awake. Assisted suicide or not, she was not going to spend hours tangled up on the floor. Margrit pressed the alarm button.

The pain arrived at just the same time as the night nurse. It was the sweet Tamil woman. She called a colleague and, together, they got Margrit back on the bed. The rest of the morning was spent in a battle with the staff and later, the doctor on call, who all wanted Margrit to be transferred to hospital. She would need to be examined, X-rays, scans. There could be a fracture somewhere, a head injury. There was certainly enough bruising. But Margrit insisted on staying put, and eventually, when the director got involved, she signed a letter confirming that she was refusing hospital treatment entirely at her own risk. However, she had to agree to cancel the day trip to Mendenswil. The director could also be stubborn.

As the morning wore on, Margrit's bruises made themselves felt despite the painkillers. She had been fairly sure she hadn't broken anything, but with the adrenaline wearing off, she was beginning to wonder. Her elbow, shoulder and hip were damned sore, the whole right side of her body really. Old people don't bounce. She had always disliked the way people talked about the elderly and falls. How it was assumed, with an undertone of satisfaction, that the person was doomed after a fall. The suggestion that it was inevitable, as if the person was a fool to ever think they would get away without falling. Well, she was not going to be the sad old case who declined after a fall. To hell with that!

When Ruedi phoned, full of concern, she had trouble convincing him that she was all right. He wanted to visit her anyway, now that he had the car booked. But he eventually accepted her wishes when she told him she would need to rest.

'Let's postpone the whole thing for a few days,' she said.

'Sure. It probably wouldn't have been so enjoyable in this heat. The weather is due to break on Sunday so we could go on Monday or Tuesday if you like. Will that be enough time to recover?'

'Absolutely.' Margrit had to cut him off in mid-goodbye because she didn't want him to hear her groan. He would put the abrupt end of the call down to butterfingers.

With a few bellows that made her sound like a cow in calf, Margrit got herself into a more comfortable position and settled down for a long, sticky day in bed – as the country sweltered under a blanket of unrelenting heat.

The one bright spot was a visit by Nadja, who had heard about the fall. But she didn't bring any judgement or sickly sympathy with her, just her usual bright, can-do attitude.

She pulled over a chair and looked Margrit straight in the eyes. 'How bad was it?'

'Well, I think the fan is beyond repair.'

'But you're still in working order?'

'Yes, sore, but look.' She flapped her arms like a hen. It hurt more than she let on.

'The nights are tough, aren't they? Last night it was still twenty-five degrees at one in the morning.' She yawned. 'I'm taking four showers a day just to cool down.'

'Do me a favour,' Margrit said. 'Go for a swim in the nearest swimming spot.'

'Oh, I don't know. Everywhere is so crowded these days. I don't go to the lake anymore.'

'So the activities woman doesn't do activities herself? Go there, first thing in the morning, or at one in the morning. Any time. Have a swim in nature. Because one day...'

'I'll make a deal with you. I'll go for a swim and I'll take a video to prove it, if you come to something on my programme next week.' She handed Margrit the familiar flyer.

Margrit scanned the list. 'Film evening. Maybe.'

'Good! By the way, your man from Depart. You seem very informal together. Am I right in thinking you know him from somewhere?'

'Yes. I know him from my young days. He lived with my parents for some time after I left home, as a foster child, you know. He was terribly shy and vulnerable. I probably only saw him two or three times, but we warmed to each other. I mean I was older, already away from home, working. So I suppose I was a bit like a big sister to him. My brothers were still at home, but they more or less ignored him. I tried to make up for that. I'm sure that was a lonely time in his life.'

'You just never know what people have been through.'

'That's right. And now, he's taking me there. Not today but hopefully next week.'

'That's wonderful! I see a change in you, Mrs Brändli.'

'Please don't say that. Don't jump to any conclusions about me.'

'I'm sorry.' She looked crestfallen. 'I'd better be getting on.'

19

Ruedi

Ruedi was doing the crossword on the back page of the TV guide when the bell rang. A short sharp buzz, Alessandra's signature ring. He looked around quickly, but there was no sign of his phone in the sitting room. Had he missed a message from her? The hall wasn't as tidy as he would have liked. He shoved the recycling bags into his bedroom and opened the front door.

'Just ten minutes,' she said. 'I'm coming from the osteopath down at the roundabout – thought I'd say hello.'

'Ciao, come in. I guess you have things for the fridge as usual.'

'You know me.' She smiled and handed over her shopping bag. Two minutes later they were on the balcony with a beer each and a bowl of paprika crisps between them.

'Everything OK at work?' he asked.

'Just some trouble with a bullying case. I'm the family's social worker. The school policy is crap if you ask me, but my hands are tied by it. Can you believe this heat?'

'Sixth day in a row over thirty degrees.'

'You didn't use the car today. I saw on the app.'

'Yeah, it was too hot. We cancelled.'

'And this old woman, who is she?'

'It's just a woman at a nursing home in Maggenried. Someone asked me a favour; it's a volunteering thing. A little drive and picnic.'

'Sounds nice.'

'Yep, well, it looks like we might do it on Tuesday instead. You said I can get a car any time.'

'Sort of. To be totally sure, let me know the day before, and I'll book one for you as near as possible. Open the app on your phone, like I showed you, and follow the steps. And then obviously you have to click "end" when you return it. I recommend you go back to the same location so you're not wandering around looking for a drop-off point.'

'Thanks again, Alessandra.'

'Look, I won't stay long. Like I said, I was in the area, and I wanted to ask you a favour as well.'

'Sure.'

'Can you take Florian for the day on Tuesday? He's in the local summer camp but there's a trip to a water park, and he hates those places so I want to keep him home.'

'You're just taking him out of the group for the day? Can you do that?'

'He's my son. I'm not going to send him someplace where he'll be miserable all day. Some boys in the neighbourhood are practically feral.'

'That's my day with the car.'

'Even better, he can see the countryside with you.'

'But this woman I'm taking, she might not be up to it.'

'Up to what? He's not a hyperactive toddler. You'll hardly know he's there, Papi.'

'It's not very convenient.'

'Well, some things are not very convenient. It's not very convenient for me to be working full time but here we are. He's a sensitive child. And by the way, what's all this stuff about the home? You gave him such a watered-down version of your life.'

The nerve! Anger surged in Ruedi's chest. 'I didn't want to talk about that stuff with him. And you already told him too much without my permission. I was forced to fill in some gaps.'

'I listened to the recording, Papi. Don't worry, you kept the mystery going as you like to do.'

'You make it sound as if I deliberately—'

'Forget it. It's your life. He has enough for his project. I have to go anyway.' She knocked back the rest of her drink. 'Thanks for the beer.'

*

The thunder that night was otherworldly, unlike any storm Ruedi could remember. He was woken by what sounded like the crack of a mountain splitting open right outside his window. The wrath of nature coming to punish all men individually.

Ruedi hadn't been sleeping well before the storm broke, thanks to several shots of schnapps he drank alone on the balcony after Alessandra left. He needed to blur the painful clarity of Alessandra's anger. He went to bed a little disoriented, his emotions alternating between maudlin and resentful. What a darling child she had been. Bright and affectionate. In an only child, the stubborn streak could be accommodated.

There were times she had complained to him about how hard it had been for her, growing up with a sick mother, having to help from such a young age. Always being sent to the shop, fetching and carrying at home constantly. *So what*, he wanted to shout. *At least you had a mother, a good mother who loved you*. She was given plenty of freedom; they never prevented her from having hobbies or going out with her friends. He didn't believe that her life had been much harder than her friends', unless their mothers acted like servants. Where was her sadness for Maria's suffering? She only seemed to see what she lost. Unless being angry at the other parent was her way of showing sadness.

The storm battered his three-storey building in a way that felt personal as the alcohol trailed through his system, wreaking havoc.

His room lit up in the beam of the interrogator's lamp, over and over. Sleep was impossible, and so Ruedi lay with these and other unwelcome thoughts churning through his mind. Finally, healing rain was the only sound, and exhaustion conquered the rest.

The last memories that paraded in front of him were of times in the home when he was first made aware of his mother's identity. There was a hierarchy, and everyone knew being a so-called gypsy was the worst. Ruedi having a mother in prison was not as bad, especially as he had made up a story about her being a bank robber, stealing from the rich to give to the poor. Some of the younger kids believed him; the others weren't so sure. Kids whose mothers had finally married and still not sent for them would have swapped places with him. But not after this day. They were messing about in the yard when a group of boys started taunting two gypsy kids. He joined in because a chant is a chant, but then one of *them*, a boy his own age, gave him a look full of spite. *Where do you think you come from, then?* Ruedi called the boy a liar and pushed him hard, but a little chime of shame inside told him that it made sense.

Years later, when he was back living with his mother, she wanted to take him with her to a funeral. One of her brothers had killed himself. It hurt her terribly when he refused to go. Apart from Aunt Doris, he had no memory of ever meeting that side of the family, and he wanted to keep it that way. By then Ruedi had started his apprenticeship and seemed no different to any other boy of his own age, poor but honest, living with his widowed mother. The thought of being seen with them, of people looking at him in that way, just when he was blending in, drove a horrible fear through him, right into his bowels. And with the fear, a familiar old companion, shame.

Alessandra was spared all that, and Florian would be too. Whether they understood or not, he was doing what was best for them. They would never feel unwanted or unworthy.

20

Margrit

Margrit rubbed a smudge off the shiny green cover with the pen clasped in her hand. Gnarled was the best word to describe that hand. Like the bark of an ancient tree. When she first discovered there was such a thing as hand cream, she had become terribly vain about those hands, even got cotton gloves to wear at night. Some nonsense she'd read in a women's magazine. With these hands, she had held her pen at school, done her chores at home, discovered the pleasures of the flesh, learned to type, dressed and undressed herself and others, carried the domestic burden, bags of shopping, the hoover, the mop, the children, the dishcloth. Endless washing, folding, chopping, peeling and polishing. Not to forget the gardening. Until they became too swollen, a good ten years ago, she had worn jewellery, painted her nails. Now she disliked these meaty paddles more than any other part of her body. The vain twenty-two-year-old was still alive and well in her.

She had done up to thirty in the audit. She started a new page.

30–39
Turned 30 in 1966. The boys were four and six.
Sense of accomplishment. Or relief? Having fulfilled my destiny.
Death of Ueli.

The primary school years. Childhood illnesses. Five summer trips to Ticino in the same holiday village. Years of watching the boys go down the same corkscrew water slide and checking that they resurfaced each time. Them wanting me to watch every time they jumped in.

Finally being able to read a book on my sun lounger when Matthias learned to swim properly.

Frederic moving to a new company further away. More money, less time at home.

Voting for the first time. Mami being so excited about it.

Peter's broken arm. Matthias falling off a tree and cutting his leg on a fence. Problems at school. Outbursts at home. Marcel's letters from exotic places.

Feeling stranded at home. Those lost hours in the afternoons. Avoiding the neighbours. Dreading the doorbell.

Sunday visits to Mendenswil. Papi getting forgetful, obstinate. The problem of the debt.

Was there a highlight? She tried to think of one. The trip to Yugoslavia for their tenth anniversary. She couldn't remember much about it. Loved the beach, didn't love the food. Frederic drank too much and talked about his work a lot.

At the end of the decade, Mother dies.

The grief back then hit her like an avalanche. She hadn't been young to lose her mother, but she'd railed against fate. She hadn't been ready to say goodbye; they were just finding each other again. She preferred the world with Mami in it, always would. Cried as if the tears could bring her back. Wandered around the farm at home weeping against every fence and tree, weeping into tea towels and old coats. Frederic took her to a psychiatrist. Her prolonged grief was some kind of disorder. The boys were upset by it. She agreed to take tablets. Life went on.

Thinking of her mother now, Margrit still felt that dogged love. What would Mami think of this course of action, she wondered. Margrit felt sure she would have understood. Even if it was unknown in her generation, and the religious part of her would recoil, she would have indulged her daughter one last time. Margrit got the message early on that her mother had a store of extra love for her; whenever she needed it, all she had to do was dip in. She needed it now. Could she still access the store? In a way, yes. In more important ways, no.

This wasn't going to get her audit done. The trouble with memory lane is that you end up falling into the ditch. Margrit massaged her writing hand and tried to place herself at forty. 1976, teenagers in the house. *What kind of music did we have then? Who was famous? Was there a war?* She couldn't remember. The only way to figure it out was to go back to the boys.

40–49

Things didn't happen to me anymore. Time moved through the changes in the boys' lives.

The decade that Matthias went off the rails. The decade spent trying to save him.

Dyeing my hair at home. The time Gianna stood behind me at the butchers and told me I'd missed a bit. Friendships petering out. Still cooking for the people anyway.

Cooking for the boys, men. Cleaning up. The time I twisted my ankle and we ate cold cuts, cheese and bread for days.

Dealing with Papi's care, the financial stuff. Trying to halt the decline of the old house. Hugo and his new wife saving the day. It was worth putting up with her personality for that.

*The times I would pull in on my way home and sit in the car
until I got cold. Peter moving out, my realising that was it, a job
well done. On edge waiting for news about Matthias. Sometimes
hoping for bad news, so the waiting could be over. The kind
lawyer who helped. Fantasising about an affair with him.*

Pottery class. My business idea. Feeling left behind.

My brothers fighting after Papi's funeral.

Weekend breakfasts with Frederic. Putting on weight.

There was something arid about those years, but one good thing
came out of the worry about Matthias. It brought Frederic and her
closer together. Having the house to themselves again did wonders
for their sex life. It was either that or giving up altogether.

50–59

*I remember this as a decade of satisfaction. I started
to spend money on nice clothes, things for the house. We
took some big trips. To Namibia, the Dominican Republic,
Canada. Frederic knew people everywhere. We went out for
dinner a lot.*

*It was too late for me to do anything with my life, or so it
felt. I stopped caring about the things I hadn't achieved. I no
longer felt the pressure of the things I should or could have
been doing – studying, reviving my career, doing valuable vol-
unteer work. I let it all go.*

*If I had landed in a country and time where my every need
was catered for, where I was safe and comfortable, why spoil
it all by feeling guilty about it?*

*New kitchen. Everyone agreed you can't expect a woman
to work in the same old surroundings for more than twenty
years. I deserved it. I went for facial treatments. Spent money
on my hair.*

Apart from the trouble with Matthias, whom I was gradually becoming hardened towards, Frederic and I had everything, and it would have been crazy not to enjoy it, at least some of the time. So that's what I did.

This was all true. But as Margrit scanned the previous pages, it still felt like a revelation to see the progression towards smugness. So many of her contemporaries had worries at that time with their parents, or their own health, or grown children still hanging around at home who couldn't get a start in life. However destructive Matthias was, at least he had taken his mess far away to another canton. He had set them free on a day-to-day basis. Margrit filled her life with purchases and pleasant experiences, and she slept soundly at night next to her faithful husband. It could have continued like that indefinitely, but there was no such thing as indefinitely.

21

Ruedi

Ruedi asked Florian to be quiet until they got to the motorway. It was good to be behind the wheel again, but before he could enjoy it properly, he had to get out of the city and away from the tram lines and cyclists. It took a lot of concentration to stay in the right lane. Luckily the air-conditioning system worked well. Much better than his old Opel.

After Maria died, he had held on to the car because of the dog. They both liked to go further afield for more interesting walks. But when all that stopped, he knew he didn't really need a car anymore, so when it failed the annual test he didn't bother with the long list of repairs and let it go.

'Can I talk now?' Florian said.

'Yes, of course. Permission to speak.' Ruedi smiled. 'That reminds me of my military service. Permission to speak, officer.'

'What else did you have to say?'

'Well, we said *jawohl* a lot and we had to salute. Like this.' Ruedi saluted a few times and Florian copied him until he got it right.

'That's very good. They'll snap you up.'

'Do they take schoolboys?'

'No, you have to wait until you're nineteen.'

'I don't know. Maybe Mami won't let me. I mean, if it's dangerous. Guns are dangerous.'

'All the more reason to learn how to use them. Tell me, did she not let you go to the water park today or was that your choice?'

They made eye contact briefly in the rear-view mirror and Florian looked down. 'I don't like to go on the fast slides. Sometimes people push people.'

The last sentence was mumbled but Ruedi understood. 'Yes, I'm afraid some people are bullies. But you have swimming lessons in school, don't you? And you go to them?'

'Yes, we go once every three weeks. You have to. I'm in the middle group.'

'That sounds good. Is that good?'

'It's OK.'

'I think it's great that you can swim. I never learned.'

'Because you were in a home?'

'No, just because there wasn't a pool anywhere nearby. There are a lot of things kids do now that they didn't do before.'

'Like what?'

'I don't know, watch TV.'

'We don't have a TV. Just the tablet and Mami's computer.'

It was nice that Florian was willing to chat. The traffic heading west on the motorway was light and Ruedi slipped into sixth gear. To his left, a train passed by, overtaking them gradually. It felt good to be on the open road with his grandson on a summer's day instead of cooped up on board in a uniform, trailing up and down the Geneva train.

'This woman we're picking up. She's very old and frail. You'll have to be careful around her. And call her Mrs Brändli – not *Du* but *Sie*.'

'I know that.'

'She's a special lady. Look, do you see the scrap heap? See all the crushed metal? That's where my old car ended up.'

'Cool.'

'Soon we'll be crossing the river and that's where canton Bern ends. Do you know what the next canton is? I'll give you a clue, the flag is black and white.'

Florian didn't answer.

'Fribourg.'

'Yeah, I know.'

'Well, why didn't you say?'

Again no answer. Florian was looking out of the window. Maybe he shouldn't have been testing the boy. They had enough of that at school.

'Just one week left of holidays. Are you looking forward to the new school?'

'Dunno.'

'I heard you're going away camping with Mami. Where to?'

'Lake Brienz. With Mami's two friends and five other kids.'

'Any your age?'

'Just a girl, the rest are younger.'

'That sounds great.'

'They're OK. A bit loud.'

'You'll be like a big family. That's fun.'

'Small families are good too.'

'That's true.'

They took the highway exit and Ruedi dropped his efforts at conversation. His mother came from a big family, people he never got to know. She was taken from her parents at the age of seven, along with two other siblings. It was part of the Children of the Open Road programme to force Yenish families to give up their way of life. He'd read about it a little; didn't want to know too much. Cruelly, the siblings were placed in separate institutions. In time the younger children were taken too. His grandmother had only managed to keep one of her babies, the youngest.

When he returned to live with his mother, she had regular visits from one sister she had reconnected with. His aunt Doris was much louder and pushier than his mother. He didn't like to see the make-up on her leathery face. At his mother's request, he would sit with them for the start of the visit until the tea was served. Then he'd make himself scarce until dinner and disappear again after eating. The sisters always spoke for hours and he would hear snatches of their conversation on his way from his room to the bathroom or the kitchen, but he didn't want to join in.

It was always the same litany of wrongs. They relived the day they were taken away, their shock at ending up in regimented care. As the evening wore on, they shared memories of their parents in the last place they had lived together. They spoke in detail about the fate of one wayward brother. Some of the time they spoke about happier times in their earlier childhood, experiences on different travels to France and back, beautiful riverbank or forest campsites, helping in the harvest, songs, parties. There were tears, remonstrations, outbursts of grief about the many dead people in their stories. Ruedi sometimes had to tell them to be quiet. He was afraid the neighbours might hear through the open window; he couldn't wait for his aunt to go home.

Doris had a ritual when she left of slapping him gently on the cheek and reminding him to look after his mother. Then she would squeeze him too tight for too long in a hug, and leave lipstick marks and make-up on his face, the kind of affection his mother would never inflict on him.

He dropped all contact when he had his own life. Shaking off the past, he'd felt nothing but relief. But now, he could see that his coldness must have hurt them both. There were things you could never make up for.

22

Margrit

It was going to be the best possible day. Margrit had ordered a picnic from the kitchen, and it was packed in a cooler box, sitting at her feet, as she waited by the front door in Sonnmatt's best wheelchair. The duty cook had even come to her room for instructions. Turkey sandwiches with lettuce, tomato and mayonnaise, boiled eggs and a salt cellar on loan, strawberries and cherries, already washed and stored in a Tupperware, a can of sweetened cream to go with them, crackers, a lemon cake and crisps for the boy. To drink, a flask of coffee and a two-litre bottle of water.

The boy. She could not remember the last day she had spent with a child. She was so curious to know him, this boy of Ruedi's. Ruedi didn't keep her waiting, of course. Always knew the right moment to appear, that young man.

He came towards her with his arms outstretched, eyes signalling pleasant surprise.

'I'm ready.'

'I can see that. Is this our picnic? And the wheels?'

'Top of the range, borrowed.'

'You're very organised.'

'Where's the boy?'

'Florian is waiting by the car. He got distracted by some butterflies.'

'Ah, a boy who notices butterflies.'

'Do you need to sign out or anything?'

'No, they know what I'm up to. The receptionist is having an electric cigarette out the back. Have you seen those gadgets? I told her I'd watch the door for her, but it's fine. Tuesday tends to be quiet.'

Ruedi picked up the cooler box. 'Do you think you could take this on your lap?'

'Of course.' Margrit took the box into her arms and tucked her handbag behind it. Ruedi released the brakes, and they headed for the door.

'I used to smoke,' she said. 'Until Usha, my sister-in-law, got cancer, and the penny dropped. I gave up from one day to the next. Terrible to think you need to see death's calling card with your own eyes.' Margrit realised what she was saying and stopped. The lavender was bowing graciously from each side as they took the path to the car park. She resolved to notice only the good things today.

The child was nowhere to be seen when they got to the car, a small red hatchback.

'He won't have gone far,' Ruedi said. 'Let's get you on board.' As Ruedi was manoeuvring the folded wheelchair into the boot, Florian appeared from around the back of the building and walked over to where Margrit was waiting in the passenger seat with the door open.

'Say hello to Mrs Brändli,' Ruedi said. 'She's brought a lovely picnic for us so you can say thank you, too.'

Florian stood shyly, looking at Margrit's knees and then his own runners, not obeying the instructions.

He looked up. 'Oh, my mask,' he said, meeting her eyes in alarm. She guessed he found her face terribly old. He pulled a mask out of his pocket and put it on. 'Mami said I had to wear a mask around you.'

Whatever you thought about masks, and she certainly didn't enjoy wearing them for all those months, they really showed how beautiful people's eyes were. Florian's brown eyes were luminous, and in his gentle gaze, she felt she could read his natural affinity for weaker creatures, including her.

'Hello, Florian,' she said, giving him a circular wave with one hand. 'You're very good to be careful around me, but there's really no need. I'm not afraid of catching anything anymore. We had enough of all that, didn't we?'

'But Mami said children are carriers...'

'Mami is very kind,' Ruedi said, opening the driver's door. 'If you want to wear it in the car, that's OK, but not when we're outside together. And if you start to feel carsick, take it off at once and open the window in the back a couple of centimetres. Now, in you get.'

They soon left Sonnmatt and the village of Maggenried behind them. The countryside still looked a bit jaded by the heat, despite the drenching it had got the other night. Margrit could not stop looking at the farms, fields, forests and livestock that whizzed past. She liked to see the well-kept homes with flowerboxes in front of the windows. It was all so pleasant and familiar, and she felt like Sleeping Beauty seeing the world again. Surely the car was the best ever invention, giving us the ability to roll through the world at speed and easily get to new places. Ruedi was a good driver, sure and steady. The boy was quiet in the back. With some difficulty she turned to look at him, and he was looking out of his window on the other side. Margrit still felt stiff from the fall and tender where the bruises were. The only parts of her body she could move easily these days were her eyes.

She was reminded of being in the car with Frederic and the boys in the early days. Apart from the ski and summer holidays, they didn't go out together all that much. The odd Sunday visit to her parents and his. So when they were in the car together there was a sense of excitement or occasion. She felt it now. The landscape around them opened up, and suddenly she could see the pre-Alps on the horizon. Her direction.

'Such a clear day,' Ruedi said.

'And a nice temperature.'

'Yes. Tell me, do you know anything about the people living in your old home now? You said it's not in the family anymore.'

'Sadly, no. Apart from Hugo, we all became city people, and his kids had no interest in keeping the place going after he died. If we had been a bit higher up in the mountains, someone might have kept it as a holiday home with a view, but who wants to go to Mendenswil? It's just an in-between place. As far as I remember, Hugo's widow sold the house to a family who keep horses. They have some kind of therapy service for children with them. At least, that's the last I heard.'

'Horses?' Florian piped up.

'I don't know if it's still the same people. Or if their business survived. But they did something for children with the horses.'

'What can horses do for children?'

'I don't know. Calm them down. Ruedi?'

'I've heard of companion dogs for children.'

'They give dogs to children as friends?'

'For children who can't communicate. Some animals understand humans very well. Especially the ones we've been living with for thousands of years.'

Florian leaned forward. 'I hope their business survived. Maybe they got money from the government, and they still have the horses.'

Children getting their hopes up, Margrit remembered now. 'Well, we don't know if the same people still live there, or if they will have time to talk to us. But we'll see very soon.'

'When will we be there?'

'Not long now,' said Ruedi. Turning to Margrit he said, 'Would you like to walk around the village first or go to the farm first?'

'Farm first,' Margrit and Florian said together.

23

Ruedi

The village had sprouted whole new neighbourhoods of one-family houses in a jumble of clashing styles. The main street was familiar to Ruedi, but he couldn't remember what turn to take. He had always gone on foot through the forest to get to school. The day he arrived in Mendenswil was his first time in a car – he remembered that. Two adults in the front, both strangers, and he was so fascinated by the dashboard and the steering wheel that he didn't really notice where they were going. The driver didn't like him leaning forward between the seats, told him to sit back. So he concentrated on the gearstick for a while until he started to feel sick. The first thing he did when he arrived at the farm was throw up on their doorstep.

He looked in his mirror at Florian, looking blithely around at the streets of an anonymous village, so trusting and untroubled. Ruedi had been two years younger when he was brought here. No explanations, no reassurances, no picnic – just delivered like a parcel to a completely unknown family in a strange place.

'Go right at the bakery. Oh, it's not a bakery anymore, it's a – what's that they're selling, Florian?'

'Candles? Bags?' Florian sounded unsure.

'Nothing as good as Waeber's bread rolls, I'm sure,' Margrit said.

'This is all new. Look at these houses! The Hayoz brothers must have made a fortune to get all this rezoned. They always knew what side their bread was buttered on, that family. There must be thirty houses here, not a single normal roof. All the lovely meadows, gone.' Her dialect was getting stronger, Ruedi noticed, the effect of being on home ground.

They cleared the last of the villas and drove through a narrow strip of forest. Coming out the other side, Ruedi finally recognised where he was. The road had been surfaced but the approach to the house was just the same, with one field sweeping down to the river on the right and a slope on the other side leading up to a crown of trees. He remembered thinning the rows of turnip plants in the big field. He remembered pulling those same turnips and feeding them to the pigs all winter. How cold and hard they felt coming out of the soil, too big for his small hands.

Their plan was to drive right up to the house and introduce themselves, to avoid any awkwardness of being caught snooping. Ruedi was surprised to see two cyclists drinking beer at a long table under an awning in the yard. A sandwich board with a price list was placed next to the table.

'Looks like they're selling drinks. Who on earth comes down this way?' Margrit said.

'Let's park and find out.'

Margrit was set up in her chair by the time a woman emerged from the house to greet them. Her jolly demeanour faded a little when she found out they'd brought their own picnic. Margrit introduced herself as someone who'd grown up there and asked how customers stumbled on the farm.

'The hiking and biking trail goes right through the yard here, so we just offer drinks, cold platters, pie, that kind of thing. Didn't you have hikers in your day?'

'Not at all. No one ever came by here. We had the road in and out and the shortcut we used to take to the village, but no one ever passed through. My father was proud that we were the last house in the village.'

'Well, if you follow your shortcut path but don't curve right into the village, you can keep going as far as Schwarzsee. It's all signposted now. And you kept pigs?'

'Yes, this building here was for the pigs, but it's different now.'

Florian stood beside Margrit and put his hand on her chair's armrest.

'Do you have any horses?' she asked on his behalf.

'No, used to, that was my daughter's thing, but she's moved over to the far side of Plaffeien.'

'Any other animals?'

'No. We're looking into getting llamas, but really we just like having space around us. I need to settle up with these gentlemen – feel free to have a look around. And if you change your minds about the menu, ring the bell on the table, and I'll be out to you. If I don't come out, I'll be stuck on a work call, so just help yourselves from the fridge and use the money box there.'

'A cat or a dog?' Margrit was hoping for some creature to please Florian.

'No, I have allergies. Feel free, enjoy.'

She hurried back into the house without inviting them in.

'Not even a cat or a dog. I thought this was a farm,' Florian said.

'Don't sulk,' Ruedi snapped.

'So much for hospitality.' Margrit wasn't sure how much she minded. Definitely a little.

'She seems busy. Let's take a look around. I could wheel you to the orchard. We'll see more from there. Florian, are you coming?'

'No.'

'What do you mean no?'

'This is a boring, stupid place.'

He spoke loud enough for the cyclists to hear, and one of them looked over at their little group with obvious interest.

'Go and wait by the car, then. And stay in the shade.'

'What a brat,' he said to Margrit when they had moved away. 'I apologise for my grandson. That's his mother indulging him all the time, treating him like a baby.'

'Oh, he's not a brat. He's just disappointed.'

'A disappointed brat.'

'Ruedi, you've met my sons. Far be it from me to give anyone advice on how to handle children.'

'But?'

'But the only thing I would do differently would be to have more patience. Yes, I think I was an impatient mother. They exasperated me. They bored me – I hate to say it but they did. Children need people who think they are wonderful. And if you don't think they are wonderful, you have to show appreciation anyway. Appreciation of their personality, their ideas – their spirit. That's what I should have realised.'

'I just believe in setting limits. So a kid knows what's acceptable and what isn't.'

'That's important too. Oh, look at the apples, it's a crying shame. These trees look like they haven't been pruned for years. Did you ever make apple juice with Mami? What a production! Do you remember that?'

'Now that you say it, I do remember making apple juice – or helping at least. There was a big old metal press with a handle.'

'And the jars. Two-litre glass jars, do you remember them? They had to be scalded first in our biggest pot. You were probably kept away from that. Do you know what I feel here? I used to think the place was a dump, couldn't wait to get away, but now I think about how industrious my parents were, the huge effort it took to keep the place going. I appreciate that. I appreciate that,' she said to the trees. 'Do you think they can hear me?'

'You're in the best place to try.'

'How do you feel, Ruedi? Does it make you sad?'

'No, it was sadder to think about than it is now to see the place. I wasn't that unhappy here. Lonely, mainly. I missed the kids, especially that friend of mine who had died. But I did feel safe with your family.'

'Thank God for that.'

Ruedi pulled down a branch, examined the fruit, and let it go again. 'I'm surprised you said that about your sons. Because you made me feel noticed when I was a boy. You showed appreciation.'

'Let's go back and find Florian. We can get your chair from the car. I know just the spot for the picnic.'

'After you,' he said, gripping the wheelchair handles.

*

'Take this and call your mother.' Ruedi passed his phone to Florian in the back. 'Tell her we'll be there in ten minutes.'

Ruedi was dissatisfied with how the day had gone, up to and including the battle he'd just lost with Margrit about paying for the car and petrol. When they dropped her off at Sonnmatt she ended up leaving a fifty-franc note on the dashboard against his wishes, which was much too much. While she was in fine fettle after the outing, the time at her old home had left him feeling drained. Having Florian misbehave was no help – all the more annoying when he should have been on his camp trip today.

He couldn't help comparing his pampered grandson, who had the cheek to talk back to the adults in charge, to how he had been at a similar age in that exact place. The very idea that he would answer back or complain was preposterous. With his own mother, he understood she had been through hard times and would never have dared to disrespect her.

Florian had been monosyllabic throughout the picnic and only defrosted a little when Margrit asked him about skateboarding. He showed her videos of tricks on Ruedi's phone. At least Alessandra hadn't bought him a phone, Ruedi thought. She had decided not until secondary school, and she was sticking to that. There were probably things Alessandra was doing right, but today's outburst showed that the boy was essentially not well brought up. Ruedi didn't believe that Florian's father would have provided discipline either – if he had stuck around. As it was, when he saw the boy, he treated him like a pasha.

When they pulled up at the parking place near her apartment, Alessandra was waiting there, dressed in beach clothes. She had a large inflated swimming ring tucked under one arm and one of those waterproof bags hooked over her shoulder. Ruedi parked and got out.

'At last! I finished work early so I could take Florian for a swim in the Aare. Here, let me scan the car key. Florian, are you getting out of the car?' She poked her head in.

'You look very summery,' Ruedi said.

'Well, it is summer. How did it go? Is he sulking in there?'

'He's probably just tired. Everything went according to plan. We didn't go inside the house, but the old lady got a chance to look around outside. She was happy.'

Florian got out of the car and reluctantly accepted a hug from his mother.

'We're going for a swim, Florian. I have all our stuff here.'

'I don't want to go.'

'What? What's the matter? What's the matter with him, Grosspapi? Why is he so grumpy?'

'He can tell you himself.'

'You're grumpy, too. Don't tell me the two of you had a row. Can I not trust you to take him out for a few hours without upsetting him?'

Ruedi stiffened. Of course, she instantly put him in the wrong. 'He didn't like the *stupid farm* because there were no animals there. The boy should have been with his friends today.'

'I hate it when you call him the boy.'

'You're raising your voice, Alessandra.'

'Florian, get back in the car for a second.' She came close to Ruedi and pointed a finger at him. 'I know what this is about. I'm trying to speak calmly, but I can't believe your attitude to Florian – and to me. I am his mother, and I decide the parameters for his well-being, so when I tell you that he is a hyper-sensitive child, you should listen to me and respect that. Do you understand?'

That old familiar arrogant tone. 'I can't hear this hyper-sensitive stuff anymore. Do you think I wasn't sensitive when I was dumped on that farm in Mendenswil as a little boy?'

'What farm? What are you talking about? I thought it was the old lady's childhood home. I thought this was your good deed of the year.'

'OK, let's just leave it. Thank you for getting me the car. I'm going to catch a bus now, and you have your swim.'

'Oh, you're walking away now. Just like you used to with Mami. Very grown up,' she called after him.

Ruedi's breath was uneven, and he could feel his body trembling. He walked around a corner and retreated into a doorway to compose himself. It was true, his way of dealing with arguments was to walk away. Maria and he hadn't fought that much, but when they did, he was so frightened of his own rising anger that he would leave the apartment rather than stay and risk an explosion.

Ruedi breathed in and out in counts of three. How he had allowed that confrontation to happen in front of Florian, he did not know. Things had slipped out of control so quickly – on what should have been a relaxing summer's day. Alessandra would hate him after this. Florian, too, probably. So much for Margrit's advice of appreciating the spirit.

Had he raised his voice as well? He hoped not. It was something he'd tried to avoid all his life. He had a horror of angry men, and he didn't even know why. Probably something to do with the time just before he was taken into care. There was so much he hadn't told Alessandra. Well, the way she went on today, she didn't deserve to know anymore. She would just use it against him anyway.

Ruedi continued on his way to the bus stop, feeling an overwhelming tiredness. It was as if he had experienced a jump forward in time to an older version of himself. He couldn't wait to get home and shut out the world. No more daughter and grandson making him feel guilty. No more Margrit Sutter forcing her will and opinions on him. No more obliging everybody.

24

Margrit

The visit home had been bittersweet. While it had been good to see the landscape again and to be reassured that the house was well kept, the soul was gone from the place. It was like a cardboard cutout of the old farm. The way of life it had embodied, the people who once gave it meaning – gone, gone, gone. Her father had sown crops and kept thirty head of pigs. Unless it was the depths of winter, you could always see and hear them when you came to the farm. They were nosy as hell, checking who was arriving. Now where were all the pigs? You never saw them in Switzerland anymore; they were raised indoors in large numbers, she assumed.

Margrit had had her early morning bathroom visit, but the health assistants were late coming back to get her dressed. It was strange to think of all the other old people in their beds, spread out over the home. All of them yearning for something, perhaps, or were they content to have care and comfort, more accepting of their lot than she was? If she remembered correctly, there were forty-five beds. She knew about a third of the residents by sight but had deliberately kept her distance. They probably thought she was deaf, and that was fine with Margrit. She didn't actually want to live here. She was just passing through for a short time. She was just tolerating the situation.

Margrit plumped her pillows and reached for her notebook. She was up to her sixties, but she didn't want to dwell on those years around Frederic's death, even if she had also been blessed by becoming a grandmother, so she decided to write about her health instead. It was hard to keep track of all the malfunctions in her body – hard to live with them, too.

High blood pressure and cholesterol, naturally. You can sort of forget about these once you have the tablets. It is the things they cause that are more troubling. 2 mini strokes so far, that I know of.

Chronic kidney disease – muscle cramps, swollen feet and ankles, shortness of breath, nausea.

Osteoarthritis, mostly in the lower back and knees.

My heart is fine. One thing the doctors are always glad to point out.

Eyes and ears – middling.

Memory – good. Miraculously, because it isn't as if I've used my mind enormously.

Digestion – could be better, see kidney issue.

Weight – a hard one to admit, but I have turned a bit barrel-shaped in my old age, and it isn't all fluid retention.

Skin – psoriasis. Pretty grim even if it is in places no one sees.

Mobility was hard to rate. On a good day, Margrit could roam the building with her walker in short spurts. On a bad day, the wheelchair was required.

Under the circumstances, a different person would make the most of their life. She had all the faculties needed to maintain relationships and an interest in the world. It was just that her people were gone, and the world did not appeal to her anymore. The culture, the politics, the behaviour – it was all so alien. Retreating into old films, music and books was a dead end. She had tried that until all the good went out of it.

In hindsight, writing a health report had been a bad idea. All that decline and degeneration. Probably why it hadn't been included in the guidelines. In fact, the whole audit idea was starting to seem misguided. It was making her feel worse.

A horrible question presented itself in Margrit's mind. Would a good person do what she was planning to do? The wish to die surely came from a dark corner of her heart, and she had given it free rein. By suiting herself, she would hurt others. She was a coward, too weak to accept the same uncertain destiny as every other poor soul. Margrit clapped the notebook shut and squeezed the covers together until her arms were shaking. She didn't notice the door had opened until the young girl from North Macedonia rushed to her side.

'What's the matter, Mrs Brändli?'

Margrit couldn't answer and she allowed herself to be soothed by the girl. Keti was her name, not Katie, she had said the first time they met. Her chestnut hair was scraped back into a high ponytail. A flawless complexion, heart-shaped face, so pretty. Another kind one. There were so many kind young people here. Once Margrit had regained her composure, Keti acted as if nothing had happened, bless her.

'I'm on my own, Mrs Brändli, but I think we'll manage fine. Sorry you had to wait.'

'It's fine, thank you. Tell me, is there a fire anywhere in the building or outside?'

'A fire? Are you cold? I can bring you blankets.'

'No, I mean an open fire, a grill or a barbecue.'

'Saturday is barbecue day.'

'Good. Are you working on Saturday?'

'Yes.'

'Can you come and tell me when the fire is lighting? I have something to burn.'

'Ah, but it is not real fire. It is electric. At home we have real fire, big parties.'

'Oh, I see. It doesn't matter.'

Margrit asked Keti to help her out onto the patio. She wondered how hard it would be to get hold of matches and a container to burn the notebook. Maybe Ruedi could help. But it would be embarrassing, too dramatic. She flicked through the written pages of the notebook. Not that many. She could burn one page at a time here on the patio and drop it on the ground. No, that would be noticed. She would be scolded. Only nine in the morning, and Margrit felt so tired. She hadn't slept well; she couldn't remember what it was anymore to sleep well.

Being at the farm the day before, she had felt the presence – or absence – of one family member in particular: her brother Ueli. He was so long dead, she honestly did not think of him often anymore. Ueli. She thought of him now. They hadn't been close when he died. She had been occupied with young children, and he was finding his way in the world. He had visited her home only once when he was working on a job in the area. At Mami's suggestion, he had stayed two nights. Unusually, Frederic was thoughtful enough to put the boys to bed on the second evening – maybe he was tired of Ueli's conversation – and she sat in the garden with her brother, and they talked about their lives. They must have had a full hour alone for the first time ever post-childhood. Back in Mendenswil, you were never really alone or one-to-one with anyone. And anyway, Ueli had always spoken the least.

She realised he admired her, the fact that she'd lived in Bern and worked in real offices. She realised he could be funny, in how he described his boss and mimicked his way of talking. It was the end of the summer, and the bats were out; he was surprisingly knowledgeable about bats. He was interested in keeping bees and was getting all the know-how by helping out a neighbour. She thought it would be nice for him to visit again – he could get to know the boys properly, be the fun uncle. The winter came and went and she only saw him in the hubbub of a Christmas visit to the farm. In the spring, he was killed in a construction site accident, and her throat was sore for the longest time afterwards with the weight of all the conversations she would never now have with him.

She realised she hadn't told Ruedi what became of her brothers. He hadn't asked. To him they must have been big lumps of young men, intimidating creatures to be avoided. The year of Ruedi, they were all still living at home and helping out around the place. Marcel would have been taking the bus in and out of town to attend *gymnasium*. The scholar, they called him. Hugo and Ueli would have been halfway through their apprenticeships, maybe military service. Her mother complained that they ate like Schwingen wrestlers, and she was tired of cooking mountains of food for them, washing their work clothes and cleaning up after them. And then one day, she had washed Ueli's overalls for the last time ever. Her grief for him had been quiet, frighteningly so. Margrit thought she must have gone somewhere to scream. She hoped so. Her father broke down whenever his son's name was mentioned. But that was all in the first years after he died. And Margrit was ashamed to admit she hadn't spent much time with her parents then, taking refuge in her role as mother, being glad of the kilometres between them that meant casual visits did not happen. Maybe that was normal. Grieving was something everyone had to do alone, in their own way.

If she were to write up her last two decades, it would be a chain of funerals, as every person she had ever known took their leave from the earth, one by one. All her aunts and uncles, her parents and their entire generation from the village, Frederic and most of his friends and family, their neighbours, cousins, the few friends she had managed to hold on to, her brothers, dear Usha, some of the younger ones she knew from her sons' generation. The bottle of grief was never empty. Always another sip to take, and another sip after that. You got used to the taste.

25

Ruedi

By the next morning, Ruedi's anger had washed away, leaving a layer of regret on every surface of his mind. It was always the same with him after any kind of confrontation and, without really wanting to, he started searching in his papers for one particular envelope marked *Nicole O*. It didn't take long to find. He sat at the dining-room table and spread out the pages from twelve years before. A newspaper clipping, his timesheet from that day, the letter from HR, the incident report in his handwriting and the official typed one he received when it was all over. Finally, inside a smaller envelope, was his personal account of the incident, which he had written for himself. He unfolded the pages and started to read.

Sunday 9 August was a very hot day and the air conditioning was broken. The passengers were all red-faced and grumpy. I noticed a woman leave her seat at the end of the carriage as I entered from the other side. She took her bags with her and did not go into one of the toilets, which I could see from the light display. I was distracted by a pregnant woman who was upset about not having water, and I had to stop and encourage the other passengers to share their water with her. Then I set off after my quarry.

People know it is actually possible to outsmart the ticket inspector on these two-storey trains by using the stairs to double back under or over a pursuing SBB employee. I didn't care enough to keep checking both levels but stuck to the upper deck, where you can walk straight from one carriage to the next. I saw her one more time, gathering her things and moving on when I came into sight. She was young, African, judging by the style of her clothes, and poor. How did I know she was poor? Growing up in poverty, I guess. You can tell. We get plenty of rich African passengers too.

That second time I saw her, from the full length of the carriage away, I could sense her desperation. Well, who was going to know? I decided to put her out of my mind and continue with the ticket-checking. The next and final stop was in fifteen minutes so she could evade me until then and leave the train. So I returned to the two carriages I'd missed and started going methodically through the passengers.

I took my break in Zurich, made a return journey to Basel, and ended up on the last train returning west to Bern. It was quiet. Some Asian tourists from the airport, a lot of lone travellers, readers, and a few harmless young people in twos or threes having cans of beer but bothering no one. And there she was again in her multicoloured dress with her pitiful plastic bags. This time she was hovering at the exit doors and bolted into the lower carriage when I came down the stairs. I guessed she would take the stairs up again and head for the end of the train I had just come from. I wasn't going to be too hard on her, but I decided to intervene this time.

So I let her get a head start, and then instead of following the direction of travel, I went back the way I had come and caught her in the middle of the carriage on the upper floor. She looked terrified and retreated quickly, bashing off other people's bags in her haste. I kept walking, feeling like the bad guy, but thinking I just wanted to talk to her, hear her out. I was prepared to be fair.

As I expected, she locked herself in the toilet. I tried talking to her through the door, but she was mumbling to herself. I hated making another person panic, so I decided this time to drop it for good. The protocol would be to call ahead for security in Olten to take her off the train. But I couldn't bring myself to do that. My mother had told me stories of being hounded by the authorities, being kicked out of places or refused entry. How could I do that to a defenceless woman? The fact that she was criss-crossing the country made me feel she must be lost, without a plan. So I carried on to Bern, finished my shift and let her do whatever it was she needed to do.

It turned out I should have made sure to get her out of there. She spent the night in the toilet. It seems the door jammed, and she couldn't get out, and in her panic, she had an asthma attack and died. Alone on the train, my train.

Later, when the investigation was under way, I did not admit that I had seen her earlier the same day on a different train. I was given a description of her, including a photo of the pattern of her dress, and it was enough to say that I had noticed her entering the toilet but that my suspicions had not been alerted. Admit nothing had been the code in the home where I grew up. And if that's really not possible, admit to the absolute minimum. It was hard to breach that, even all those years later.

I haven't told Maria about it either – she's not so well at the moment. I am too ashamed. Yes, I wasn't the first ticket inspector to knock off duty without combing every inch of the train. And I wasn't to know that the cleaning team had been delayed and that the train would go onto the sidings without a full check. But I should have known that she was in desperate straits. Chasing and then giving up just made things worse. This time, taking the stern, formal approach would have been the right thing to do. Security would have handed her over to the police, who would have handed her over to the immigration authorities, and somewhere along the line, she would have had the chance to ask for help – instead of being stuck alone on a train with her terror. Nicole, no apology will make any difference to you.

There was a police investigation, but ultimately no one had done anything they could be prosecuted for. Because she was undocumented, there was no family or embassy pushing for answers. Our internal inquiry didn't want to pin the blame on anyone and even the journalists weren't that interested in writing about the case. People felt bad, or said they did, but it was seen as just one of those unfortunate things. If no one else feels guilty, it has to fall to me. Someone has to care.

That was it. His pathetic testimony. He made it his duty to read it from time to time, but he had never worked up the courage to show it to anyone else. How did he end up becoming one of those people in authority that the weak were afraid of? It didn't sit right. It just didn't sit right.

26

Margrit

Peter was due at seven. Margrit asked to be taken outside and parked under the chestnut tree around the corner with a table and extra chair. The new Ukrainian woman in the kitchen was the only person free to set her up, and it took some sign language to get everything just so, especially the jug of water, syrup and glasses.

Peter followed the instructions in her text and found her outside. He leaned down to give her a kiss. 'Are you warm enough out here, Mami? It's not high summer anymore.'

'I'm fine – look, I have my blanket and my cardigan. Nobody uses this side of the garden, I don't know why.'

'The other side has the view, I suppose.'

'Nicer planting here. How are you, Peter? How's work? Nathalie?'

'Work is changing all the time. Lots of meetings about new systems. They won't let anything be.'

'Human nature.'

'Well, my nature is to want to be left in peace to do what I'm good at.'

'You were always very independent at play, do you know that? I used to see other children dragging their mothers into their little games, and I was so grateful that you were self-sufficient. And then, of course, Matthias came along, and he could be your deputy.'

'I don't remember playing much with Matthias.'

'There was a phase when he was old enough for you, and you weren't too old for him. But it's true, it didn't last long.'

'Don't forget that Matthias broke everything he played with, even supposedly indestructible toys. He was a handful, wasn't he?'

'How is Nathalie?'

'Getting over her eye operation. Strangely, she's very upset about your plan. Too upset to come and say goodbye, she says.'

'That is strange.'

'I don't mind. I mean, I'm trying not to mind.'

'Considering how critical she has always been of me.'

'The feeling is mutual, right, Mami?'

'We're not a natural fit, that's all. I'm sorry about that, by the way. I know it made life complicated for you. But there aren't that many people in life we truly connect with, are there?'

'I'd like to think that you feel connected with me.'

'Pour us both some syrup – it's elderflower.' She smiled at him. 'You are a good son, Peter. Always have been.'

'Someone had to be.'

'You're my first child. I loved you completely when you came into my life, but I found mothering difficult. Being alone with you, being responsible for your every need. Those damn weighing scales we rented from the pharmacy. And all the instructions. The things that were meant to make me sure made me unsure.'

'What weighing scales?'

'In those days, we were told to weigh the baby before and after each feed and then to top up with formula if you didn't reach the target. Everything was supposed to be perfect. Percentile this and percentile that. I think they were trying to help us with all the check-ups and measurements, but for me, it created intolerable pressure. When my brothers were babies, my mother just felt our backs to know if we had a fever. In my day, we had to track your temperature hourly when you were unwell.'

'That does sound heavy. Do you know something? You're more talkative these days, since the decision.'

'Should I be quiet?'

'That's not what I'm saying. I like to hear your memories. It makes me wonder if the conversation is really finished. What happens when I can't ask you anything more?'

He made a noise between a cough and a laugh. Margrit realised it was a sob.

'Peter, please. This will happen anyway. It happens to everyone. At least this way you can be ready. Tell me things, ask me things.'

'In just over a week!'

'We have had a lifetime together. Please let that be enough.'

'I'm sorry.'

'I'm sorry for not being more open. I kept things to myself. That's my way. I'm the eldest – I tried to solve my own problems. I'd like to think I did my best for you. From the very beginning until now. You have a busy life. My role was to set you free to lead that life.'

'It just felt like you weren't interested.'

'Let's not get upset. You're right, it's got cooler. Shall we move inside?'

Peter's eyes were red, but he kept his composure for the rest of the visit, for which Margrit was thankful. She guessed other mothers loved to see that raw old need in their grown children, but she did not. She wanted them to be fine without her.

They even managed to talk about the last day, and Peter accepted that it would be better for him not to be there in the final moments. For both their sakes.

Margrit pulled her blanket up a little. 'I have a feeling Matthias won't come, and I understand that. I don't think either of us ever thought he'd outlive me. He tried his best not to. I hope you can understand if he doesn't come, and forgive him. You should have whatever support you wish for on that day, even Nathalie if she's up to it.'

'But I don't want Meret to be there,' he said.

'Yes, I understand your decision.'

'And we're going to tell Luna afterwards. She's so far away from home.'

'Will you tell them the whole truth?'

'I'm not sure. Maybe later.'

Margrit had thought her granddaughters would gravitate back to her one day, but it hadn't happened. They had so much going on in their lives – who could blame them? She took a piece of folded paper from the pocket of her cardigan.

'I've written down some of my funeral wishes. Music and so on, what to order at the restaurant afterwards.'

Peter tucked the paper into his jacket pocket and lowered his head.

'Tell me all about New Zealand,' she said, willing him not to cry.

27

Ruedi

On his way to meet Carmen, Ruedi still felt the effects of the row with Alessandra, though two days had passed. His stomach was unsettled, and there was a strange tremor in his breathing. He was failing at family, and it felt terrible. All the mean thoughts he'd had about them made his heart twist with regret. Alessandra and Florian were all he had left. Any other people he was related to by blood, including the second set of kids his father had had in England or the people his mother had been taken from as a child, did not count as they were strangers.

This time he arrived early at the Generationenhaus, and he got them a table. Carmen was meant to check through his final preparations, and she wanted to check on him, she said, make sure he was holding up all right.

He took out his phone for the hundredth time. He wanted to text Alessandra, but anything he thought of to say sounded pathetic. She really didn't respond well to clichés. She needed something truthful and convincing from him. He gave up again. If he could skirt around some of the story, he might be able to ask Carmen for advice.

She arrived late and flustered. A person at the train station had had some sort of violent breakdown on the platform. The public had been herded back to use the exits at the other end of the station. Carmen had heard the man's heart-rending cries.

'You would think I'd be used to it from work, but this man sounded so horribly distressed and out of control. Everyone was subdued. Walking away as fast as they could.'

'How awful for you, Carmen.'

'Well, I didn't see anything. You must have seen your share of incidents working on the trains.'

'I only ever felt afraid a couple of times. Once trying to prevent a racist attack, and once when I was face-to-face with a very unstable young man with a knife. In general, I got through difficulties by being non-confrontational. In my employee assessment interview every year, I was evaluated for crisis management, and my superiors always made the same complaint – that I was too soft.'

'That I can imagine. Not that I see it as a problem.'

'Thanks. You get all sorts on the trains – youngsters in high spirits, mentally disturbed people, messy drunks, men preying on women passengers, and people generally having a bad day. Deliberate fare evaders annoyed me the most, especially if they looked like they could afford to pay. I was brought up to respect rules and pay my way.'

'And different approaches work with different people. That's what I find in the prison.'

'Yes, some respond to a stern approach, but others need gentleness. And sometimes we get it wrong.'

Carmen looked at him keenly. She took a sip from her cup. 'Are you all right? Is the case getting to you?'

'The case is going fine. Mrs Brändli trusts me. We had our outing the other day, and it went well. She's easy company.'

'But you're not getting close?'

'We are having interesting discussions, that's all. She has things on her mind now and not many people to talk to.'

'Yes, I've had that too with clients. Do you have any questions for me?'

'I don't know. I've given the police advance warning of the time. How long do you think I'll have to stick around afterwards? And the sons, will they have to stay there too?'

'Yes, you will need to stay until everyone else has given their statement, the doctor especially. It could take up to three hours. Depends if the police have done it before. The sons are not your responsibility but I'd expect them to stay. Have you informed the undertakers?'

'I'm about to – I just have to get the older son's OK on which company to use. Is it still strange to you, making all these practical arrangements, planning a death?'

'Yes, it's still strange. But when the police leave, make sure you leave, too. You don't have to stay to hold the hands of the family. I find people can be overdependent and expect you to take charge of everything. Especially when it's a parent, and the offspring never learned to lead in the family context. Let them take ownership of the situation – gently, obviously.'

'Gently.'

He leaned back, and Carmen mirrored him. 'Ruedi, do you mind me asking if you grew up with any Yenish traditions? You mentioned your mother being Yenish.'

'She was taken into care pretty young. I think she was careful not to pass anything on to me.'

'It's just that I saw a flyer for an event that's coming up in Fribourg. It's an open day organised by the Yenish community, a bit like a fair. Maybe that could be interesting for you.'

'I'm not in the community – I have no contact.'

'Sure, but if you wanted to discover—'

'I don't see myself going to a fair like that. It really has no connection to my life anymore. I mean, thank you for the suggestion but no, it doesn't appeal.'

'And your daughter? Is she interested in her roots?'

'She would be the type, but she doesn't know about all that ancient history. It's better that way.'

'And your father, what was his story?'

'My father wasn't Yenish. He left my mother when I was a baby. Went to London, had another family at some point, or so she heard. He had no involvement in our lives, and his family showed no interest in me either. So that's a closed book.'

'That must have been very tough for your mother. And yet she held on to you and brought you up. An impressive woman, I'm sure.'

'She did her best, let's say. I still spent most of my childhood in care.'

'Oh, I didn't realise. I'm sorry, Ruedi. You never know what people have been through.'

'I don't know if I had the best preparation for fatherhood. Maybe Alessandra is right, and I haven't been a good father to her.'

'Did she say that?'

'Not in so many words.'

'You've been there for her all her life, haven't you? Even now, you help out with your grandson. You provided for her and got her set up in life. Surely she acknowledges that?'

'It wasn't easy for her having a sick mother.'

'I can imagine it wasn't easy for you either. Can she imagine that? You know, I have very little patience for people who still blame their parents for things far into adulthood. Do they think they would have done better? Don't they see that you're only human? It makes me glad I don't have children.'

'I can't believe we've spent the whole time talking about me and my regrets. Sorry for burdening you, Carmen.'

'I don't mind at all. It seems to me that you still have some things to work out. I'll only make one recommendation, if I may. From what you describe, life taught you to be closed, to the extent of hiding things. And yet here you are today, being open with me.'

'That's because you have a gift. Or maybe you're a saint.'
He smiled.

'The gift is being open. If I had a prescription pad, I would
write on it: *Open up*. Beginning with Alessandra.'

28

Margrit

Margrit turned the postcard over in her hands. The photo showed an aerial view of a bay with the words *Nha Trang* across the bottom right-hand corner. So she had made it as far as Vietnam. Luna's message was short and generic, and it took Margrit some time to decipher the English words *island-hopping*. It could have been a postcard from any girl to any relative, but Margrit was undone by one phrase: *See you in November!* And the kisses, a whole line of kisses.

Keti had brought the card to Margrit at the breakfast table. On a whim, she had decided to make her way over to the dining room that morning. Table for one. Maybe she wanted to show that she still could if she wanted to. That she wasn't hiding anything. And now, here she was out in the open, exposed, with tears in her eyes. One by one, the other residents left and it was just Margrit and one of the kitchen staff, moving closer as she cleared the other tables.

With trembling hands, Margrit moved her plate out of the way and placed the card, text down, on the table. Luna would not see Margrit in November. She would never see her grandmother again. And one day she would know that Margrit had chosen things to be that way. Eight months earlier, when Luna came to say goodbye before her big trip, Margrit hadn't yet started thinking of Depart. It was still winter and she had some vague idea of not wanting to go through another one. That's how it started. From ruminations about hating winter to the realisation one night that she could actually escape and never see its dominion again. But when Luna came to visit, she hadn't got that far yet. She had been poor company, she remembered, suffering from one of her regular urinary tract infections. It didn't matter, though, because Luna was in full flow of excitement about her big trip and all Margrit had to do was smile and absorb it all. Luna wrote down the places she would pass through on her journey, a string of meaningless words. Margrit enjoyed her vitality, her shining eyes. It was like seeing someone in love. But the glow faded the minute Luna left the room, and Margrit could have screamed in frustration when she wet herself in the bathroom before she could struggle out of her tights.

Margrit accepted help to get launched on her walker. The catering woman wasn't curious about her tears or her name, thankfully. She obviously had to get through her duties before lunch. Making smoother progress than usual, Margrit walked back to her room, trying to ignore the card sitting in her basket, weighing nothing but loaded with accusation.

She put the postcard in the drawer of her bedside table and it struck her that she didn't have a photo of Luna or of Meret. Why hadn't Peter brought her any? Why hadn't she brought one from home when she moved? Probably because they were used to sending photos by phone these days. She settled in the chair and opened up Peter's messages on her phone. She scrolled until she got to a cluster of photos sent in May: Luna in mid-air diving off a pier, Luna smiling while sipping a cocktail, Luna looking back over her shoulder on a forest trail carrying a huge backpack, Luna on a scooter, Luna on a rope bridge, Luna in the water. She looked happy, but how real was any of that? The world as a playground. It reminded her of Nathalie and her showy escapades.

Luna had always been feisty. She would attack a playground like a little soldier, scrambling to the top of every structure, swinging off the highest bars, running with the zipline to reach the fastest speed. If other children got in the way, she pushed past them. Observing her in action one day, Margrit absent-mindedly commented that Luna was just like a boy, but for that she earned a lecture from Nathalie about the harm of stereotyping girls. There was no point in Margrit saying that she was glad Luna was strong and fearless. She wanted her to be like a boy in the hope that it would give her an easier path through life.

Luna would be all right. It was Meret who took things more to heart. Meret of the tender embraces. The child gave the most loving hugs. But there had been no hug for many months. Margrit hadn't been well enough to attend her younger granddaughter's school graduation. Before that, Meret had been busy with her exam preparation; later came the language course in Sicily and, this last month, a job serving in the café of the local swimming pool. Margrit scrolled forward, looking for more photos. She was sure she had one of Meret receiving her Matura diploma. And there she was in June, standing in between her parents, almost as tall as her father, a playful smile on her lips, as if she knew what a cliché the image was and had no intention of continuing with such a conventional life. At least that's what Margrit saw. Despite her sensitive nature, Meret was a free spirit who would surprise them all. If only she'd had a chance to talk to her about her plans, she was sure Meret would have understood. When she found out, if she did, she would grieve but she would understand.

Yes, Meret was the one who would cry the most for her. But it was too late to summon her here, wasn't it? That would just make it harder for both of them. Especially when her parents thought she was too young to be involved.

Margrit came across another, more recent photo, one she hadn't realised Peter had sent. Meret at the pool café in a T-shirt and shorts, wearing a cap and balancing a tray of drinks on one hand.

She was waving a finger at the camera and scowling, obviously not happy to be photographed at work. Peter was lucky to have them. What a wonderful consolation for him.

The girls had reached such an interesting age and Margrit was deeply sorry to have to give up the privilege of following their progress. She was certain they would make something better of their lives than she had, maybe even break through the heavy, safe canopy of Swiss life and breathe free air. What she wished for them was a greater life – not in terms of kilometres away from home or fun experiences, but greater in that they would know their own potential and put it to good use.

29

Ruedi

Ruedi squeezed through the dining-room chairs in the hall to get to his phone on the kitchen counter. Unknown number. He dried one hand on his trouser leg and answered. Matthias Brändli sounded different on the phone – polite. Ruedi almost hung up, assuming it was a telemarketing call.

'Look, I don't want to bother you, but maybe you can help me out.'

'What is it you need?'

'Just some advice.'

'Go ahead.'

'Well, as you can probably see, my mother has a very low opinion of me. At one time, I gave her good reason, but that was years ago. Since I got on the methadone programme, I have made unbelievable progress, baby steps and all that, but I live an upright life. I feel like I have atoned for what I did, but she has never acknowledged the stuff she did. And she has kept me at this cold distance for my entire adult life, regardless of how I have tried to make amends. I mean, I got therapy. I was the problem person, and everyone agreed that I needed therapy – but she would never admit she needed to face up to things about herself.'

'She's an eighty-six-year-old woman, Matthias, very near the end of her life. She is making her own preparations, but that is something between her and her conscience. You must see that the moment for having things out with her has passed.'

'So you're saying I should leave her alone?'

'I don't know what you're asking. You said you wanted some advice.' The sitting-room floor was dry now, and Ruedi started carrying the chairs back to the table with his free hand.

'Well, strange as it sounds, I want my mother to respect me. Especially now. She likes you. I think if you spoke to her about how well I'm doing, she might realise. You could tell her I have lived in the same studio apartment for seven years. I get up at four in the morning to deliver newspapers. I have responsibilities in the building: I sweep the leaves and clear the snow. I help in the Caritas shop, and I keep to my budget every month.'

'Those are things you can tell her without accusing her of anything. I'm sure she'd be interested.'

'She's never visited me here or anywhere I've lived. I just want...'

'What do you want?'

'Some honesty. I want her to admit that she shut me out. That she never forgave me.'

'Well, it's not my place to force your mother to admit to any wrongdoings. I am not her priest or therapist.'

'But you are an advisor of some sort. Did she tell you that I have a son? When I found out about my son, I made an effort. I tried to be in his life. OK, it didn't work out, but she had no interest. Didn't even want to meet the kid. What am I supposed to do with that?'

'You said you wanted my advice. Go and see her – but soon. And be conciliatory. Tell her how well you are doing and that she doesn't need to worry about you. You could say sorry, you could say thank you. Now is the time to be understanding, to make peace. It is better to be sorry for the missed years than to be angry. My most important advice is to please leave anger at the door when you talk to her. It is too late for all that.'

'I suppose you had a good mother?'

'Yes, I did. We had our challenges, but she was a good mother to me.'

'And you were a good son.'

'I tried to be.'

'I was not a good son.'

'If you put her first now, you will be.'

'I did love her. I do.'

'Well, maybe that's what she needs to hear now. Keep it simple. Now, I must go – goodbye.'

He placed the last chair at the dining table and sat down on it. Now that the floor was clean, he noticed the dust everywhere else. Half of the table was covered with paperwork. He couldn't remember the last time he'd had to clear the table to serve someone a meal here.

He picked up the phone again and searched for Alessandra's name in his messages. The most recent messages were about borrowing the car and dropping it back. She had ended the last one with an emoji of a face blowing a love-heart kiss.

Alessandra used to love his *Älplermagronen*. Ruedi knew there was something wrong in the way he often reacted to Florian. Maybe there was something wrong in how he reacted to his daughter too. Margrit had talked about patience and nurturing a child's spirit. Carmen prescribed openness.

Hello Alessandra, I'm sorry about the other day. Thanks again for the car. Please come to dinner, you and Florian. Macaroni at my place, tomorrow or the next day? Greetings.

He deleted the word *greetings* and, with a bit of scrolling, found the kiss-blowing emoji. There was a first time for everything.

30

Margrit

This will be my last diary entry before I burn the damn thing. The audit is over – not entirely pointless, but ultimately not that helpful. I did not manage to uncover any great truth, no single wrong turn or right turn. I am glad that no one will be subject to my scribblings.

Matthias turned up today wearing a suit. He didn't even wear a suit to his father's funeral. He looked like an actor in a cheap play, a bad actor. He started wittering on about his apartment, and I think he was trying to invite me there. Apparently, he keeps to his budget. He gave me a breakdown, and it does seem very low, but so are his outgoings. I reassured him that he would get his full share of the inheritance and that should make his life easier, but he got agitated and said he wasn't trying to ask for money. There is no way to make that man happy.

He said he will come next week on the day and do whatever I ask. He started talking about his spiritual beliefs, some kind of amalgam of Mother Nature and Buddhism, and I listened for a little while. I appreciated one thing he said about life as a river flowing into the sea. We are all one substance evaporating and falling again. But if that were really true, no one would ever be lonely.

All the same, this theory of flow and renewal is something I can accept much more easily than any kind of divine order. If there was ever any design behind this valley of tears, the dogs ate it.

I am not afraid of dying. With the drug I'm taking, I know death will come efficiently and without trauma. Endings are sad but unavoidable. There comes a night when your mother bends to kiss you goodnight for the last time. You do the same with your own children. You stop without even noticing because it is natural to stop everything one day. It will be like that.

All the pain can be left behind like a pile of clothes on the beach. The love I received I take with me as a final blessing. The love I gave is long gone, and for that I am sorry. I hope it counted for something.

Margrit was reading back over the last paragraph, cringing a little at the note of self-pity, when the door swung open and Nadja appeared on the threshold on crutches. She closed the notebook and pushed it under her pillow.

'What's all this? I heard you were off sick.'

'I've come to check on you.'

'I'm fine, never better.'

'Really?'

'Really – the bruises are impressive, but no real damage. But what happened to you?'

'Volleyball. Wrecked my knee for good this time. Well, they won't know for sure until the swelling dies down and I can get a scan, but my gut feeling is not good.'

'What are you doing here? You should be resting!' Margrit gestured to her to sit down.

'Martin drove me in. He's having a coffee with his uncle, a resident. I had to collect my laptop and sign some stuff – it's quicker in person. So I came to say hello.'

'That's very kind, Nadja. When did you have your accident?'

'The day after you. It's the damn heat. The floor was wet from sweat, I reached for the ball, and my leg went the wrong way. In training! More fool me for carrying on for so long.'

'What do you mean?'

'Mrs Brändli, I'm the oldest one there. I'm past it, even for the third league. It's embarrassing.'

'Like my story.'

'Yes, we're both a disgrace. But it's a miracle that you didn't break anything or dislocate anything.'

'You could say. That storm the other night felt like a miracle, too. Nature does what it wants.'

'Nature is telling me to stop playing volleyball.'

'Don't look so sad. You're as fit as a fiddle or will be soon again. If it's not volleyball, some other sport.'

'I don't know. Volleyball has always been my game. And my next big birthday is fifty. I don't think the options are that great.'

'Fifty! You are going to be in your prime for another twenty or more years. You can replace volleyball – you can even replace that knee if you want to. This isn't like you, Nadja. Where's your positivity?'

Nadja shrugged. 'I get tired, too.'

'Poppycock. You know what I regret? I regret every day I got up during all the years I was fit and healthy – like you – and I did nothing with that gift. Or I did the wrong things. I kept the house clean only for the dust to settle and the handbasin to get limescale all over it again a day or two later. I prepared meals that took too long to cook and were eaten in five minutes. I spent time with people I wasn't interested in. I didn't even earn any money. My actual best years. My body and mind were strong, and my will was passive. The only thing I was good at was killing time.'

Nadja started to say something but gave up.

'What could I have been doing? That's what you're wondering,' Margrit went on. 'I could have mastered something. I liked the sciences. So it was never encouraged in school – so what! I could have taken courses, or taught myself from books. Anything, anything in the world. I stagnated. Spent my prime waiting for my husband to come home. What an enormous waste.'

'If you feel that strongly, I'll go back to volleyball.'

Margrit laughed. 'I'm scaring you. But look at these legs, these useless legs. I used to be so strong. Like you. I could have climbed mountains.'

'We can't all climb Everest.'

'What you do is wonderful. I'm getting carried away. The truth is this doesn't apply to you. The things you organise, the encouragement you give others. When your knee heals, you'll be just as amazing as ever.'

'Well, thank you. I also know of old people doing big things, by the way. Have you read about the retired women taking the climate case to Europe? It's clever. They're organising, they're fighting back. Not just leaving it to the young ones.'

'I haven't heard about that. The news is too much for me. I had to stop once and for all when we had that tsunami. No more wars, plagues, disasters – I can't take it.'

'Get your phone, read about those climate women. Read about the new clean-energy stuff if you like science. There are good things happening too.'

'Aha, so the positivity is still there.'

'Still there, I guess. Sorry, Mrs Brändli, I have to go. I get another two weeks off for this. Don't go anywhere before I get back.'

'I can't promise anything.'

'But you still have time, don't you?'

'Let's talk about that when you get back.' Margrit feared her voice would betray her, but Nadja seemed untroubled. She stood up and got her crutches in position.

'Take care. No more sudden moves, all right?'

'You take care, too. Thanks for everything, pet.'

Nadja looked at her strangely. She hesitated, as if she wanted to say something, but she turned to go. Feeling wretched, Margrit reached for the notebook again and started pulling out the pages.

31

Ruedi

Älplermagronen reminded Ruedi of Maria, because she used to pretend to be scornful of the dish. She would put on her parents' accent and say, *This is why Swiss people should not be allowed near pasta*. But it was one of Ruedi's few staple recipes, and all three of them had second and third helpings when he made it.

The macaroni dish was in the oven, and he was just opening the can of apple sauce when the bell rang. At the door, Ruedi took out the guest slippers he kept especially for them. Florian's were on the small side, but he didn't comment. Time to go up a couple of sizes.

Alessandra had a few things in her handbag, and she asked if she could put them in the fridge.

'You must be Migros's best customer,' he said as she handed him some cream cheese and ham.

'Least efficient customer, more like,' she said with a wry smile. 'I was much better organised during Covid. Had my list for the week, and I made sure to think of everything. When I was a kid, we always had the same things on certain days of the week, remember? Now that's real meal planning.'

'Your mother was well organised.'

'A lot of meals have been cooked in this kitchen.' She opened the oven and peeked at the macaroni. 'It's going to dry out. Did you not think to cover it with tin foil? Here, I'll take it out. Florian, come and get the things to set the table.'

'The table is already set. Alessandra, you're the guest. Why don't you pour yourself a glass of wine – see, I have a half bottle of red open there – and go on through? Florian, you take in the water jug, and I'll bring the food through in a minute.'

When they were onto second helpings, Ruedi asked Florian how he had got on with his family history project.

'I got a five.'

'Wow, that's great.'

'He'll show it to you next time you're in our apartment. It's a PowerPoint presentation, and he did a very nice job with old black-and-white photos of Switzerland he found online.'

'You do projects on the computer at your age? That's very impressive.'

'You wouldn't believe it. They are real little corporate monkeys. More than ready for *Sek*.'

'Florian in secondary school already! I can hardly believe it.'

Florian made monkey noises, and they all laughed.

'I know it's a school night and you can't stay long, but while I have you both, can I just say that I'm sorry for being cross the other day? I'd like to explain something.'

They both looked at him in expectation, identical eyebrows at a matching angle, a mirror image of each other.

'Maybe it would have made sense to explain this to you in advance, but we don't always do things the right way round in life, do we?'

'Grosspapi, I'm sorry for being rude.'

'That's all right. It wasn't that much fun for you, I'm sure.'

'No, I liked the drive and everything. I liked the old lady, too.'

'Yes, she's a nice person. Well, the thing is that I lived in that exact place when I was a boy. It was a real working farm then and I was sent to live there when I was ten years old. I went there from the home, and it was a strange change for me, confusing and lonely.'

'Papi, you don't have to talk about this if it upsets you.' Alessandra reached out her hand.

'No, I'd like you to know more. The good thing is that my mother found me there, and with the help of some kind people, especially a woman called Vogelsang who gave us a place to live, she was able to get me back. After eight years apart. And your grandmother, Alessandra, she was so overjoyed to have you in her life. She was a great help to us.'

'But she died.' Florian frowned.

'Yes, she died when your mother was already grown up and working. She was very proud of us, wasn't she?' Ruedi turned to Alessandra.

'Yes, always. She was a home child too, wasn't she?'

'That's right. And I'll tell you more about her story another time. Let's get this cleared up, and you can tell me about your camping weekend. I haven't seen any photos yet.'

32

Margrit

She hadn't thought she would sleep at all, but here she was, waking on her last day in Sonnmatt. The objects in her room came gradually into view in the pre-dawn light. The desk and one dining-room chair were the only furniture she'd taken with her from home. She had hardly sat at the desk since she got here. It had become little more than a shelf for the post and Frederic's photograph. But it was pretty, and that was why she'd kept it.

Other people were living in their family house now. Renters. It was a family of two women with kids from previous marriages who were now a couple. It must be nice to share a home with a woman, Margrit thought. Less cooking, more to talk about. Using the desk as a portal, Margrit went to visit the house as it had been in the early days of their marriage.

She gets out of her marital bed and walks to the door, laying her hand on the tall chest of drawers that contains their clothes. Frederic is there behind her, his solid sleeping form a comforting presence. On the landing, she pauses to admire how the faintest shadow of the birch tree spreads a pattern on the floor. How old would the boys be? She can't tell yet.

Peter's room first. He is lying still, head to one side and still small enough to carry, though she does not carry him anymore.

In the next room, Matthias stirs as she comes in and scrambles to his feet. He holds on to the side of the cot as she bends to kiss his cheek. His arms encircle her neck, and when she straightens up he is wrapped around her in his favourite place. She sways with him, and he lays his head down on her shoulder and yawns. It's still early. They can be sleepy together.

When Margrit woke again, it was bright, and someone was speaking to her. She opened her eyes, and there was Kalpita, the Tamil woman with the soft voice.

'Good morning. I never saw you sleep so late before. Breakfast time is almost over. We have to hurry. Coffee, bread roll, jam?' She helped Margrit sit up and fixed her pillows. 'Let me pass on the message, and I'll be back in a minute to take you to the bathroom. Oh, and Keti asked me to give you this.' She took a photo from her front pocket, handed it to Margrit and bustled away. Everything seemed so normal. Margrit was glad to have a moment to collect her thoughts.

So she had missed a full hour of her last day. The bubble of normality was about to burst. Above all, Margrit wanted to keep her composure. She was already putting everyone to enough trouble, and she didn't want to add an old woman's tears to the burden. Her bladder was uncomfortably full. Her legs ached. The body, always imposing its failings and functions. Good riddance, she thought, and suddenly she had to laugh at the ridiculousness of her situation.

When she was spruced up, Margrit put on her newest nightie and a pale blue cardigan that was nice and light. Without being asked, Kalpita dusted and straightened everything and left the patio door open a fraction to air the room. Margrit had decided to spend the morning in bed and receive visitors like a patient. A hummingbird of nerves hovered between her stomach and her chest. Soon, they would start to arrive.

Just as the Angelus bells clanged in the distance, Peter came first with Nathalie. She looked haggard, or maybe that was just age catching up with her. Matthias was only a few minutes late, and the director came in with him to shake hands with everyone. Ruedi appeared last to call them in to lunch in the private sitting room. They all cleared out and Kalpita came back to help her dress.

At lunch, everyone was very gentle with her. Something funny had happened to Margrit's concentration, and she missed half of what they were saying. They ate filet mignon, and Margrit enjoyed it even though she was dealing with the thought that the food would never be digested. The human mind was capable of accommodating any level of strangeness, she now knew.

Peter had the most difficulty keeping the tears at bay, and Margrit noticed Nathalie squeeze his hand and pat his back from time to time. It didn't really fit with her perception of her daughter-in-law, but it was too late to care about that. The boys had a nice conversation about Margrit's cooking, mentioning their favourite dishes, how they used to go straight to the cooker when they came home from school for lunch, and cheer when they saw what she had prepared. Ruedi said very little. He had to leave the room twice to take calls or speak to someone. Not that the illusion had been very robust, but it was feeling less and less like a normal lunch. Matthias put his head in his hands at one point, which was briefly horrifying. Then he apologised and carried on.

The plates were cleared by a new member of staff Margrit didn't recognise, a thin man with a goatee. She felt perversely glad she wouldn't have to remember his name or be nice to him. Her sons declined dessert, but Margrit wanted the last thing she tasted to be strawberries and cream. She said no to coffee. Nathalie handed out cups from the coffee machine in the corner, and the others took sad sips with their eyes cast down.

There was less than an hour to go. Margrit would have liked to freeze everyone with a magic wand mid coffee-drinking and use the same magic wand to transfer herself back to bed with only professional people around her. But the goodbyes had to be faced.

33

Ruedi

The doctor was waiting back in her room, but Ruedi hesitated in the corridor, reluctant to interrupt Margrit's leave-taking from her family. He looked at his watch for the hundredth time that day. Thirty minutes to go. Throughout the meal, he could tell everyone was using all their will not to look at their watches. Ruedi always cleared everything off his plate out of training, but he would gladly have skipped that meal if he could have got away with it. The Brändlis were a defunct family. Perhaps the father had been the glue that had held them together. What was taking so long?

Finally, he knocked and entered the sitting room. Margrit was sitting in one of the armchairs, and Peter was kneeling at her feet with his head on her knee. She rested a hand lightly on his head, but Ruedi saw she was dry-eyed. Matthias was standing at the window, looking out. Nathalie was not there. All three looked at him with different emotions engraved deep on their faces. Ruedi, the Angel of Death. He swallowed hard, indigestion burning his chest.

'We should get ready,' he said, turning to fetch her walker from behind the door.

Peter rose with all the weariness of an ancient martyr. He helped his mother to her feet. Both sons came close, towering over her. Matthias put his hand over hers and Peter copied him. They were blocking the way, and Ruedi saw the effort it took to step aside and let her leave the room. He didn't look at the men but busied himself guiding the way and holding the door. He heard the rhythm of hard sobs about to break before he closed the door.

While the doctor prepared the patient, conducting a short, unnecessary examination, Margrit looked small and fragile. Ruedi felt his heart contract with concern for her. He fought the urge to shout *Stop*, imagined himself throwing the doctor out of the room. But Ruedi made no sound. This was what it was all about, and there was no room for anything but professionalism and love. Because at that moment, it was clear to Ruedi that he did love Margrit. That the natural response to a fellow human being in the shadow of death is love.

The director, Balsiger, sat in the corner with a grave expression on his face. Margrit gave Ruedi a card for Nadja and a small plastic bag full of torn-up paper to dispose of. Her husband's photo had been moved to the bedside table, and tucked into the corner was a snapshot of a girl in a baseball cap carrying a tray. Margrit asked him to describe the place where she grew up. He started stumbling through a rather unpoetic description of the location, and she smiled her encouragement.

'You've been more than kind to me, Ruedi. Thank you for everything. My thanks to all three of you. Don't worry, this ordeal will be over soon. I see we're ahead of schedule, doctor. I'm ready.'

The doctor handed Margrit the paper cup.

She looked at Ruedi. 'Live well, my friend. My sons will ask if I had any last words or wishes. I was not great company at lunch. The truth is I haven't been great company for the larger part of my life. All I can say is I think I went astray, and I don't know why. That's not very satisfactory, but it is common! If they could remember the good times, remember me with love, that would be good for us all.' She sighed. 'Enough now.'

Margrit swallowed the drink and lay her head back on the pillow with her eyes closed. Ruedi held his breath. Her hand flew to her throat, and she gave two great gasps before settling. Ruedi released his own breath and watched the gentle rise and fall of her chest. Minutes went by as Margrit's presence faded. The stillness in the room was immense while they waited for the doctor to react. He was counting the seconds on his watch. No more seconds for Margrit. But Ruedi was proud of her. Courage, dignity – to see it close up like this.

The director stood next to Ruedi as the doctor checked for a pulse. There was no priest, no ritual to fall back on. Death was in the room, no doubt about that, and soon the business of death would begin. There would be demonstrations of grief, important phone calls to be made, forms to be filled in, and the unescapable fact of the body left inconveniently behind. The doctor nodded at him, and Ruedi reached for his folder. He knew what to do.

Epilogue

A week later

In a field next to a broad and shallow river, an outdoor gathering is taking place. There are food stalls selling the usual things: waffles, churros, veal sausages and bread. A folk band is playing on a small stage, and people mill about, looking for something to admire or buy. A boy watches as a craftswoman burns letters spelling out *GROSSPAPI* onto a leather bracelet. It's a present for the boy's grandfather – he wants to cheer him up. He's never bought anything for an adult before in his life. A dog tied up in the shade looks like he would be glad of some company, but the boy is too cautious to approach him. There are lots of dogs here today, which has been the highlight for him – that plus paddling in the river. The people around him keep switching from French to German and back again. The music is a bit different to the usual traditional stuff. Faster, twistier. He feels foreign in this French-speaking town, even though he's only half an hour from home.

He left his mother at a book stand, her bag stuffed with leaflets, talking to a woman who had written a book about her life. His grandfather is sitting at a picnic table with an old woman friend whose name is Carmen, drinking beer. To think he cycled all this way. But they were going to get the train back together.

He notices the boy looking and holds up a can of Coke for him as an invitation to come over. It is odd that his grandfather has friends these days. Like that lady in the car the time they went for a picnic. The boy had only ever seen him alone before then. Well, if his grandfather can make friends at his age, maybe *he* will be able to find new friends in the new school. He hopes so.

The boy pays for the bracelet and goes to the table where he left his churros. The gift brings tears to his grandfather's eyes – he's been emotional on and off all day – which was not the boy's intention. But his grandfather puts the bracelet on straight away and says he'll keep it forever.

Acknowledgements

Despite the title, this book is a product of winter. Two winters in a row, I worked on the manuscript, first encouraged by my daughter Ashley to finish what I'd started, and the next year guided by my wonderful editor Laura Shanahan to add breadth and depth to the story. Without them, this novel would not have come to life.

Many thanks to Louise Boland, Greer Claybrook, Beccy Fish, Amy Blay and all the team at Fairlight Books for giving *Before the Leaves Fall* the best possible home, alongside my first novel *Voting Day*. I'm grateful to Deborah Blake for copy-editing and to Charlotte Norman for proofreading.

From the first draft all the way to publication, my family have been fully supportive. Heartfelt thanks to Thomas, Maeve, Ciara and Ashley Zbinden, and to Máire, Helen, Ruth, Dirk, Thomas, Ali, Fintan, Aoileann, Cian and all the O'Dea clan.

Kim Hays and Ben Moore played a vital role in the early stages of this book, for which I am very grateful. They and other fellow writers have helped me keep the faith. Special thanks to Alison Anderson, Michelle Bailat-Jones, Caroline Bishop, Padraig Rooney, Emmanuel Tagnard, Kathleen Peters, Tasja Dorkofikis, Jeannie Wurz, Julie Hunt and Deirdre Coghlan.

About the Author

Originally from Dublin, Clare O'Dea has lived in Switzerland for two decades. She studied French and Russian in Trinity College Dublin, and has had a varied career in the Irish and Swiss media.

Her first novel, *Voting Day*, was published by Fairlight Books in 2022, and is loosely connected to *Before the Leaves Fall*. Clare has also published three non-fiction books: *The Naked Swiss: A Nation Behind 10 Myths* (2016, with an updated edition in 2018), *The Naked Irish: Portrait of a Nation Beyond the Clichés* (2019) and *All About Switzerland* (2024, ebook).

Clare grew up in a bilingual home speaking English and Irish. She now lives in the bilingual (French/Swiss German) town of Fribourg with her family.

CLARE O'DEA
Voting Day

In February 1959, Switzerland held a referendum on women's suffrage. The men voted 'no'.

In this powerful novella, Clare O'Dea explores that day through the eyes of four very different Swiss women. Vreni is a busy farmer's wife, longing for a break from family life. Her grown-up daughter Margrit is carving out an independent life in Bern, but finds herself trapped in an alarming situation. Esther, a cleaner, is desperate to recover her son who has been taken into care. Beatrice, a hospital administrator, has been throwing herself into the 'yes' campaign. The four women's paths intersect on a day that will leave its mark on all their lives.

'A vivid, fascinating snapshot of a recent (almost unbelievably recent!) moment in Swiss history. I devoured it in one sitting.'
—Jonathan Coe

ALLAN RADCLIFFE
The Old Haunts

Recently bereaved Jamie is staying at a rural steading in the heart of Scotland with his actor boyfriend Alex. The sudden loss of both of Jamie's parents hangs like a shadow over the trip. In his grief, Jamie finds himself sifting through bittersweet memories, from his working-class upbringing in Edinburgh to his bohemian twenties in London, with a growing awareness of his sexuality threaded through these formative years. In the present, when Alex is called away to an audition, Jamie can no longer avoid the pull of the past: haunted by an inescapable failure to share his full self with his parents, he must confront his unresolved feelings towards them.

In spare, evocative prose, Allan Radcliffe tells a wistful coming-of-age story and paints a tender portrait of grief in all its complexities.

'Equally heart-warming and sorrowful. Each and every sentence has been artfully penned... a pleasure to read'
—The Scots Magazine

'There is much to admire in this novel: the elegance and economy of the writing, the understanding of emotional difficulties, the truth to life'
—The Scotsman